2/24

DEADFALL

DEADFALL

Cynthia Harrod-Eagles

Chivers Press
Bath, England
•
Thorndike Press
Thorndike, Maine USA

This Large Print edition is published by Chivers Press, England, and by Thorndike Press, USA.

Published in 1999 in the U.K. by arrangement with the author.

Published in 1999 in the U.S. by arrangement with Dorian Literary Agency.

U.K. Hardcover ISBN 0–7540–3715–0 (Chivers Large Print)
U.K. Softcover ISBN 0–7540–3716–9 (Camden Large Print)
U.S. Softcover ISBN 0–7862–1827–4 (General Series Edition)

The text of this Large Print edition is unabridged.
Other aspects of the book may vary from the original edition.

Set in 16 pt. New Times Roman.

Printed in Great Britain on acid-free paper.

British Library Cataloguing in Publication Data available

Library of Congress Cataloging-in-Publication Data

Harrod-Eagles, Cynthia.
Deadfall / Cynthia Harrod-Eagles.
p. cm.
ISBN 0–7862–1827–4 (lg. print : sc : alk. paper)
1. Large type books. I. Title.
[PR6058.A6945D34 1999]
823'.914—dc21 98–11722

For M.G.: Solomon, 5:16

As for man, his days are as grass:
As the flower of the field, so he flourisheth.
For the wind passeth over it, and it is gone;
And the place thereof shall know it no more.

Psalm 103 vv 15–16

CHAPTER ONE

She dreamed that she had woken up, and the man was hanging over her again, standing beside the bed and leaning down close to her face—oppressive rather than menacing. She heard him say her name, urgently as if trying to wake her. Then she did wake, and for a recognizable second after she knew she was awake he was still there, a blackness blocking out the light, and she screamed, waking herself properly.

For a while she lay still on her back recovering. She was sweating lightly, and she could feel her heartbeat fluttering erratically all over her skin. It was not that the man himself seemed threatening, but it was the fact of him, and the fact of that terrible moment of overlap into reality. There was a man in the bed beside her and for the moment she could not remember who it was. Easy enough to find out, but she would not let herself turn her head to look. That was the worst thing about this recurrent dream or vision or whatever it was, the sense of disorganization it left her with. For a few moments after she woke properly she was always disorientated, could not remember where she was or who she was or when it was, and the blankness in her brain, where that simple information ought to be, filled her with an indescribable terror.

The man had not woken when she screamed, but he stirred now, and the slight movement released a little puff of warm air from under the duvet that brought the smell of him to her nostrils. Her frozen brain unlocked and remembering streamed gratefully in. It was Joe Thomson, whose refined friends called him Elephant Whang. She rolled over against him and slid a hand down under the covers. His eponymous organ stretched in her palm welcomingly and he groaned in his sleep.

'Wake, you bugger,' she said pleasantly. They say that the most instantly comforting thing for a human being is to have something in your mouth. She knelt up over him and dipped the upper half of her body so that her left nipple touched his lips, and his mouth unfolded silently and automatically like an RAF inflatable rescue dinghy and closed again over her breast. Or in someone else's mouth. 'Miz Scarlet,' she murmured, 'I has tol' you an' tol' you—'

'Whattimzit?'

'You don't really want to know that,' she said, kneeling astride him. Still only half awake he brought his hands up to her hips, lifted her, fitted her down carefully and precisely over his erection. She was wet with fear, and he went in smoothly and she sighed with comfort and relief and he woke properly.

'You been dreaming again?'

'Mmm.'

'Must be some dream to get you worked up like this,' he said thoughtfully, after a minute.

'So modest, EW?' she said after another minute. He was a mechanical engineer with astonishingly delicate hands and fingernails in perpetual mourning. And, of course, the non-woolly comforter. Dreams receded before his solid reality, and afterwards she settled in the crook of his arm and slept soundly until morning.

* * *

'Was that you ringing my doorbell last night?' she asked Polly. It was mid-morning and they had met in the ice-cream parlour in Fulham Road.

'Mmm,' Polly said through her straw. 'I was passing on my way home and saw your light on. You were in then?'

'Oh yes.'

'Bad girl. Who was it this time? Another of your lorry drivers?'

'Nostalgie de la Banlieu,' Agatha said.

'If old Phil could see you now, eh? You've certainly had your revenge on him, anyway. How many since he left you?'

'Lost count,' she said indifferently.

'Scarlet woman,' Polly said.

'He made me one,' Agatha said. 'It was his name, remember.'

'Yes, of course. You were the Woman with No Name, weren't you. A sort of Cunt Eastward.' She contemplated the level of her milk-shake critically. 'It must be really exciting being an orphan.'

'I don't remember much about it,' she said.

'No, but really. I mean you could be anyone. Whereas I—'

'Can only be someone,' she finished for her. 'Still, at least you know who to blame.'

'My mother,' Polly said darkly.

'For running off with another man?' Agatha said, raising an eyebrow. Polly looked indignant.

'It's not the *sin* I minded,' she said. 'It was the bad taste. He had dentures and wore suede shoes.'

Agatha grinned. 'I bet you didn't notice that at the time.'

'At least your mother died tastefully. Not to say romantically—imagine being pulled out from under the rubble in the Blitz as a week-old baby. With your advantages you ought to have become a great actress or a best-selling novelist.'

'But you forget—my father probably ran off with a woman with peroxide hair and a taste for mauve chiffon scarves. Bad blood will out.' She bent down to retrieve her handbag from the floor. 'Have you finished?'

'I don't believe you ever had a father,' Polly said. 'That's too ordinary. Your mother wasn't called Mary by any chance, was she? Oh no, of course, you were named after her, weren't you?'

'That's one thing your mother didn't do for you,' Agatha said.

'Yes, Polly's quite a decent name. Where are you off to now?'

'Guildhall, and then the dentist this afternoon. No, I'll get it. Have this one on me.'

She led the way down to the cash desk and out into the sunshine. Polly came along behind her, and on the street said, 'Hey, Ag, did you know you're going grey?'

'I'm not surprised, with those dreams I've been having,' she said lightly.

'No, really, there's a big streak at the back here—turn round—here. Wait a minute.' Agatha, head bent, a hank of her back hair in Polly's hand, waited patiently. 'Turn to the light,' Polly said peremptorily. Agatha turned, carefully, mindful of her roots. 'That's funny,' Polly said. 'You aren't turning grey at all.'

'I'm very glad to hear it.'

'You're turning blonde.'

'If you say so,' Agatha said patiently. Polly was offended.

'No, honestly.' She inspected the hair again. 'I suppose it must be the sun bleaching it. Funny that it should go in a lump, though.'

'Never mind. I must go, Pol, I've got a pupil. Ring me tonight?'

'Okay. Have fun.'

*　　*　　*

Her pupil was waiting for her in the entrance, and she thought she must be late until he called out to her, 'Hello! It was such a nice day I thought I'd wait here, not waste the sunshine.'

'You should be warming up,' she told him sternly. He grinned engagingly.

'Plenty of time yet. It's not even twenty past.'

'You're looking very smart,' she said, changing her case from one hand to the other. It was heavy, being full of fat American instruction books. 'Going somewhere?' He was dressed in white Oxford bags and a pale blue blazer, à la Gatsby. On anyone else, she reflected, it would have looked terrible, but he was eighteen, slender, elegant, and poised between Eton and Balliol, and social confidence sat gracefully on him.

'Not particularly,' he said, turning to fall in alongside her as she headed for the stairs. 'It was an attempt to keep up my morale.'

'Oh,' she said. 'Things bad at home?'

He made a grimace. 'I wish they'd just get divorced and be done with it,' he said. 'Only they stay together for my sake, and ostentatiously don't quarrel. It makes me feel such a burden. If they'd only ask me, I'd tell 'em.'

'You don't look like an unwilling recipient of charity,' she said, reflecting how simple relationships look from the outside. 'You look positively privileged.'

'You know my methods,' he said. He paused to open a door for her, and caught her eyes in a significant gaze as she went through. 'I need all the help I can get to get through a lesson with you.'

She wasn't sure what he meant. With a male ten years older, she would have known, but he was more or less a child. Wasn't he? She frowned, assuming the role of teacher in self-defence.

'You mean you haven't practised again?'

'Oh yes, I've practised,' he said.

'But not enough.'

'You wouldn't think so,' he said. She wouldn't be charmed.

'Now look, Gerry,' she said, and he interrupted quickly,

'Oh yes, I know, when you were my age you practised ten hours a day.'

'It's true,' she said indignantly. 'You'll never get anywhere if you don't love it more than anything else in the world. The trumpet's a hard master.'

'Yes, I know,' he said restlessly, 'only—when the sun's out—and they keep on and on being polite to each other—I just can't seem to make myself do anything but lie in the garden. I don't even read. Don't you ever feel like that,

Agatha?'

Using her name was a direct appeal. They went into the practise room, and she put her case on the table and hid her face by busying herself getting out her instrument. No, she thought, I don't. That's one thing that can never be recaptured once it's gone, that divine indolence. Other attributes of youth can last, or be rediscovered, the curiosity, the energy, the optimism; but the ability to do nothing, nothing at all, for hours on end, once gone is gone for ever. She felt, abruptly, every one of the years she had over him.

'Well, come on, let's get warmed up,' she said briskly. 'I want to hear what you've been doing. And then—' she pulled out *Der Wustling* and slapped it down on the table.

'Oh no, not Stravinsky,' he wailed, but she could see he was pleased. He had great talent, and if his parents' problems did not disrupt him too much, he would go far. She pulled her mouthpiece out of her hip pocket, where she kept it for warmth, and took herself into a corner, ostensibly to warm up, but in reality to observe him warming up. In two minutes he had forgotten her presence, and his eyes—great dark blue eyes fringed with long curly lashes—were absent and stern with concentration. She could understand why the parents stayed together—not because they thought their parting would harm him, but because neither could bear to give him up.

Afterwards she praised him for working so hard, and he grinned with delight and said, 'Since you're so pleased with me, would you let me take you out to lunch?'

'I can't,' she said absently. 'I'm going to the dentist.'

She must have sounded more brusque than she meant to. His cheeks burned with confusion and he said, 'Well, I didn't mean necessarily today. But—'

She felt sorry for him, and exasperated because he made her feel so old. (Going grey? No, Polly had said it was blonde. Not possible, surely? Must be going grey.)

'Well, I'd love to have lunch some other time,' she said as kindly as she could. He pounced, eagerly.

'Tomorrow? Please say yes. I know just the place. You'll love it.'

'All right,' she said, and then, trying to be gracious, 'thank you. But now I must get going. And you—' She levelled a finger at him, and he reached out and grabbed it.

'I know,' he said, smiling. 'Practise!' It was a childish, affectionate gesture, but she met his eyes and was suddenly embarrassed, feeling his maleness for the first time. She pulled herself free abruptly and left.

* * *

The dentist looked hot and bothered, and

smiled at her with relief.

'Ah, hello,' he said. 'I'm glad it's you. At least I know you won't be any trouble.'

'Had a hard day?' she asked, sitting on the chair and lowering herself cautiously into its leather embrace. He waited for her to lift her legs on, and then jacked her efficiently down.

'Terrible. And so hot. I've showered three times already.'

'Are your armpits your charmpits?' she said.

'Only just. But some of my customers have the gobs of slobs. And children—!'

'Refuse to do them,' she suggested.

'Professional ethics,' he said. 'Who am I to refuse? Anyway, here *you* are, and I can relax for five minutes.'

'Is that all you're going to give me?' she said indignantly.

'Sorry.'

'And after getting me horizontal. Oh well, I suppose it's just the teeth as usual.'

He grinned. 'Any trouble since last time?—no. I hardly have to ask you. A better, tougher set of gnashers I've never seen. Does it run in your family?'

'I haven't got any family. My mother died when I was born, and my father never came back from the war.'

'No brothers and sisters?'

'Ungch!' she said through his fingers, and when he withdrew them, 'I was a one-off effort.'

'Oh well. Maybe it's a blessing,' he said, holding her x-ray up to the light and studying it. 'I've got two brothers and we all hate each other cordially. When did I do this x-ray? Was it last time?'

'Ungh ingh ungleugh,' she said.

'The time before last? So it's just a year old. Right, let's see now.' Propping it up where he could see it he filled her mouth with little steel tools and pink clean fingers and began to poke about, humming to himself. The humming didn't last very long. He probed the upper right molars, looked at her card, and said, 'Hello! you've lost a filling, haven't you?'

'Unf,' she said, a split second before he added, 'No you haven't, though. This tooth has never been filled. I must have looked at the wrong—' He checked back on the chart, looked into her mouth again, and said, 'No, it was that one. That's funny.'

'Something wrong?' she asked, taking the advantage of his digital absence.

'Not with your teeth,' he said reassuringly. 'It's just that they don't match your record card. I must have got the wrong card. Nurse!' But even as he called, his expression grew more puzzled. 'It's got your name on it all right,' he said. 'And the x-ray—'

The nurse came in, and he took her away into a corner. They examined the chart together, talking in undertones, and then came back to her.

'You call it out to me and I'll go over them,' the dentist said. Alarmed, Agatha submitted to his fingers and probes again as the nurse called out the dental work from the card and he went over her teeth one by one.

'And that's all,' the nurse said, looking up hopefully. The dentist removed his fingers again.

'Well they don't match at all. It *must* be the wrong card.'

'But it can't be,' the nurse said patiently. 'The name's written on, and it hasn't been altered. See for yourself.'

'I can see,' he said irritably. 'The fact remains—'

'Look, would you mind telling me—' Agatha said. He recalled his charm.

'Sorry,' he said, smiling. 'Administrative cock-up. We seem to have the wrong card for you—'

'It *isn't* the wrong card,' the nurse said crossly. 'Look, it says Mrs Agatha Scarlet on the top in letters an inch high—'

'Nevertheless,' the dentist overrode her firmly, 'there must be a mistake somewhere. Your teeth,' he told Agatha, 'don't match up with the work recorded on your record card.' He looked at the nurse again, and his charm faded a little. 'You don't suggest that Mrs Scarlet's teeth have changed?'

'Oh these are the ones I got out of the glass this morning all right,' Agatha said cheerfully.

'All I know is—' the nurse began belligerently, prepared to defend her system to the death.

'Never mind. We'll have to make up a new card. You take down as I call out.'

The nurse went off to fetch a blank, and Agatha, looking at his suppressed irritation, said, 'It's your fault for saying you'd have no trouble with me. That was tempting fate. And if you go on seething like that you'll have a heart attack, or ulcers.'

He smiled unwillingly.

'I'm sorry about all this,' he said.

'I don't mind,' she said. 'It gives me longer lying here in your arms. Your chair's arms, I should say.' She watched with faint amusement the speculative look flicker across his face. Under the skin, they're all brothers, she thought, even dentists. But he was too professional to ask her out. Fortunately, since she might have been tempted to accept. And she already had to go and have lunch with Gerry tomorrow, which was just about as awkward as it well could be. The nurse came back with the blank record card and an injured expression, and Agatha abandoned herself to ten minutes without the need to think. She was glad that the dentist was being vigilant on her behalf, knowing how important her teeth were to her, but she wished he wouldn't tick off the nurse in front of her. She didn't care about the deficiencies of his system, as long as her chops were up to standard. With the Strauss Alpine Symphony coming up tomorrow—rehearsal from ten till one and concert at eight, and recording sessions all the rest of the week—she couldn't afford any breaches in the dam.

* * *

She was struggling up from an immense depth of sleep, swimming upwards as though through deep water towards the surface. When she broke through, she found herself in a strange room, in bed, staring at the wall opposite, a wall she had never seen before. It was low-ceilinged, and papered in a brownish paper with tiny flowers all over it. Where the hell am I, she thought, panicking. She didn't know any room like that. She didn't know where she was.

And then she knew he was beside her, standing beside the bed, looking down at her and calling her name.

'Agatha,' very softly, 'Agatha, wake up!'

That's it, she thought, I'm still asleep. I'm dreaming this. Otherwise how could I know in a dark room that the wallpaper is brown? He leaned over her, and she saw his face, a face which, though she had never seen it before, was familiar to her. She felt his hand on her shoulder, and then the cold air as he drew the sheet back from her, and as his face hung lower over her, and the familiar fear came again, and she thought I must wake up properly. She tried to struggle up through more water, but there was no sensation of waking. Only, quite suddenly, like a bubble popping, the room was her own room again, and—

And he was still there. She screamed, shrilly, and she was alone, awake, and cold. The sheet was down off her shoulders. Lying still, recovering from her panic, she thought it must have been the sensation of cold that triggered off the dream. It must have been a dream, because now she could not remember what his face had looked like, though at the time it had been so vivid.

She lay still, trying to redefine the barriers between dream and reality, and then the phone rang. It was Polly, and she was weeping.

'Oh Ag—'

'Darling! What is it? Is something wrong?'

'Are you alone? Can I come round?'

'Now? Yes, of course. But what's happened?' Premonition. 'Is it Paul?'

'He's left me.'

'Oh God.' A familiar, sinking feeling. 'Well, come round and tell me about it.'

'Oh, bless you, darling Agatha. Oh Ag, I'm so unhappy.'

After she had put the phone down, Agatha got straight out of bed and put on her warm dressing-gown (as distinct from her smart dressing-gown, which was almost exclusively used for seeing gentlemen callers to the door late at night) and padded downstairs to put the kettle on. Polly sounded pretty bad. She would be here in five minutes—she only lived down the road. Poor Polly. But, Oh Lord, rehearsal at ten tomorrow, and the Alpine Symphony, and Oh Lord squared, lunch with Gerry, and then the concert, and EW said he would come round afterwards. She was glad that Polly had immediately thought to turn to her, but on the other hand Polly was nine years younger and had her grief to keep her awake. Yawning, Agatha cursed her ambivalence, and sat on the kitchen chair to await the kettle and the doorbell, tucking her feet up under her and shivering sleepily.

CHAPTER TWO

Dressing, heavy-eyed, trying to adjust to the day which felt already congealed round her lethargic mind; grabbing the nearest things to wear, trousers to save having to put on tights, and the blouse she had worn yesterday; tripping over the trouser legs and discovering that the waist swam round her. Jesus, I must have lost some weight—these used to be tight on me. Too long because too big, she would be tripping herself up all day. Then she remembered, she had to dress up a bit anyway because of lunch. Few things worse than undressing again and having to choose something else. Trying to unseal her eyes she groped about in the wardrobe and in desperation pulled out a pinafore dress.

With a white blouse it would pass. Tights, damn it—legs not yet brown enough to go bare. And of course, tights put on in a hurry always went squint, so that when they got to the top of the legs the crotch missed by inches and the centre seam boldly went where no seam ought to have gone before. She tugged feebly, then trying to twist the legs round put both thumbs right through the fabric.

'Shit!' she said, collapsing on to the edge of the bed. She caught sight of her reflection in the mirror, shackled around the knees by torn nylon, and her sense of humour reasserted itself. 'Shit to the power of ten,' she said, and with a lopsided smile hauled the bloody things off again and threw them across the room. 'Now, start again,' she said to herself, 'and this time keep calm. Nothing is gained by getting cross.' She looked at herself again in the mirror. 'What the hell—?' She stood up abruptly and went over to the glass and stared, not really believing it. She put her hand up to her head, and watched the reflection move as if she expected it to stay put. To the right side of her parting was a lock of blonde hair, and there were smaller streaks on the other side. She reached for the hank of hair and pulled it forward, squinting upwards at it. It was too short to get a proper look at, but as Polly said, it was definitely blonde, not grey.

But it hadn't been last night.

People going grey overnight from shock.

People who have heart attacks go grey in hours sometimes.

Blonde?

It wasn't possible. *Was it?*

Her mind revolved around the impossible possibilities. She even went to inspect her pillow, sniffed it for the smell of bleach, scratched it for paint. Then she stood for some time, staring at the mirror but not seeing, wondering what was happening.

'Something hormonal?' she asked aloud, and then grinned. Poor old hormones, get blamed for everything. Well, it was too early for the change yet, and besides, she had never heard of anyone going blonde with the change. And besides again, it was after nine o'clock and the rehearsal started at ten and if she didn't go now this minute—

She flung down the stairs, grabbed her case and scooted breakfastless out to the car. If the traffic wasn't too bad she might have time for a cheese roll and a cup of coffee before rehearsal started, although she didn't like to play after eating or drinking because it made the mouthpiece smell funny but whatthehell archie whatthehell. In the car automatic pilot took over and she relaxed, her released mind going back to Polly, who hadn't left until going on four this morning, swollen-eyed and exhausted. Poor kid! Telling her,

'He said he didn't want to hurt me. He kept saying it, and all I wanted to do was scream at him, don't do it, then.'

He had treated her badly from the beginning, Agatha thought, stringing her along, never committing himself and yet expecting her to commit herself. Willing to take everything from her, her company, her time, her sympathy, her body, but giving nothing in return, and excusing it by saying I don't want to get involved.

'Why don't they realize,' Polly saying, 'that they *are* involved, from the first moment? They're like kids crossing their fingers and saying fanelights. It doesn't count if you've got your fingers crossed.'

Agatha remembered. What was this new terror men had, that had grown up since she had grown up? Women had changed, of course, so perhaps it was inevitable that men should have too—but why in that particular way? Women, now greedy for themselves, their own lives, coming up against this emotional black hole, that sucked everything in and released nothing. Polly saying,

'He kept telling me that he never promised me anything. And that was true, but he didn't seem to realize it didn't help.'

You promised me nothing and by God that was the one promise you kept. Agatha remembered her own husband Phil, leaving her in much the same terms, after five years of not realizing they hadn't been married to each other at all. Where were you all that time, Phil? Where are you now? I couldn't find myself, so it isn't surprising you couldn't find me either. But every act of seeking myself reaffirms my identity, and the more myself I grow the less I can be anyone else. How can I be myself without building layer on layer of *me* between me and the rest of the world?

Phil saying, 'You don't love me, you know. You never did.'

Herself saying to Joe (though it was said to reassure him), 'I am too full of will to love.'

Self-will, refusal to be annihilated, determination to be oneself—they took the place of love. Did men, before the revolution, feel like that, and did women make up for it by loving them against all odds, despite themselves, through everything? And now no one is willing to compromise, and we are all alone.

'What will become of us?' she said aloud. The lorry driver in the vehicle alongside her, waiting at the traffic lights, grinned and winked at her, and she smiled back to excuse her moving lips. Only on that level we can still meet—me and Joe for instance—as long as neither of us takes it seriously. She felt suddenly very, very tired of it all. What's happening to me? She looked at herself in the rear-view mirror and with renewed shock saw the blonde streaks.

Not possible.

The lights changed and she moved off again. Go to the doctor? All right, some time. But now—too busy. Strauss. And breakfast, oh please be time for breakfast I'm so hungry so tired black coffee stimulant Strauss is one hell of a big blow but oh *lovely* he knew trumpets all right tackatackatacka tacka-*ta* tacka-*ta* tee-dum yadda-dum. And what was that bit—

* * *

Jim Blackburn was there, Gerry's father.

'Hello petal,' he said when he saw her. 'Long time see.'

'You always did have a great line in repartee, Jimbo. How are you? What are you doing here?'

'Bumping,' he said succinctly.

'What on earth for?' Agatha said. They were strolling towards the platform, last on as always, brass section the manager's despair.

'Well, money of course. You don't think anything but money would induce me to bump up Malcolm Tyzack, do you?'

'You don't need money,' Agatha said disbelievingly. 'You with a son at Eton?'

'Scholarship boy, don't forget,' Jim said indignantly. No musician likes it to be supposed he's not hard up. They threaded their way between the cellos and basses, and Malcolm and Bill, first and third trumpets, scuffed their feet in ironic applause for them. 'How is that brat of mine, anyway?'

'Don't you know?' Agatha said.

'I don't go home more than I can help,' Jim said. 'It gets a bit hairy at home, you know. I'd sooner keep clear.' He passed behind Malcolm to get to his seat beyond him, resting a hand on Malc's shoulder to balance. Malc pretended offence.

'Gerdoff, yer fuckin' arsebandit,' he said, threateningly. Agatha took the seat on his other side. 'Come on, Aggie, get yer finger out. We want an early finish today.'

'You must be kidding,' she said, flipping open her music. The tangle of notes jumped about the staves like disturbed ants. 'Je-sus I'm tired.'

'Been doing it in again?' Malcolm asked with scant sympathy. 'No wonder you play like fuckin' rubbish.'

She looked at him and smiled disarmingly, and his eyes gleamed in response. He always acted the hard man to disguise his soft heart, afraid he'd get stopped by every begger and flag-seller in the street. 'Go on, you lying old sod,' she said pleasantly. 'You know I'm the best second you ever had.'

If Jim hadn't been home much, and didn't know how Gerry was, he wouldn't know how upset he was either, or that he wasn't practising, or that he had asked her to lunch. Perhaps she shouldn't talk about him. Gerry, at eighteen, began to be entitled to his own life and his secrecy, didn't he?

'Thank you gentlemen,' the conductor said, cutting through the chatter and warming-up noises. 'We'll start with the Strauss.'

They played. Oblivion here, at least; concentration, absolute, and the music, not a function of theirs, but a thing in itself, existing outside them, into which they tuned with more or less success. Not so much as if they played it, but as if they channelled it through from another plane, made it audible. Nothing but the music—

Yeuch! Something wrong. The conductor dropped his hands, they straggled to a stop. Something bum there.

'Again from twenty-four,' he said, lifted his hands, and—ough! Malcolm kicked her leg, hard, and she yipped like a puppy.

'It's a fuckin' b natural, not a fuckin' b flat, yer stupid tart,' he muttered out of the corner of his mouth.

'Trumpets,' the conductor said mildly. 'Someone isn't playing the accidental.'

'Sorry,' said Agatha, scarlet.

'Yer fuckin' blind?' Malcolm asked, angry because upset.

'Sorry,' she said, to him. But yes, she had missed the squiggle, it looked like a smudge on the paper. She pulled her stand an inch closer, and found herself leaning forward to see. What was wrong with her eyes? Late night, eye strain, or was she getting short-sighted, curse of musicians? They played it again, right this time. At the next pause she tugged her stand forward a bit more, and had to play at an angle to clear it with her instrument. Oh God, oh God, at least cubed.

Coffee break, and Malcolm nipped out with her, slipped an arm round her waist and said,

'Ey, y've had yer hair streaked. I like it. Except the bloke that did it must be as short-sighted as you.'

'You are a rotten sod, Tyzack. If you weren't so brilliant you'd have no friends,' she told him.

'No, but honestly, are you having trouble seeing?' he asked, and his hand at her waist expressed sympathy and concern.

'I haven't noticed it before,' she said. 'Just this morning I can't seem to focus. And before you ask, no I wasn't doing it in last night. I haven't had a drink for over twenty-four hours.'

'You must be mad.'

'No, I think it's just that I'm getting old.'

'Join the club,' he said, pushing her ahead of him into the bar.

'I wouldn't belong to any club that would have me as a member,' she said.

'I wouldn't belong to anyone that would use my member as a club,' he said. 'Come on, you old ratbag, I'll buy you a coffee. Only you'll have to lend me the money till we get paid.'

She edged herself into the queue and slumped against the wall. Malc was a sweetie, but she couldn't tell him about her hair. It sounded too bloody silly.

'Are you in the queue, Malc? Will you get me one?' Jim asked, coming in after them.

'Agatha's buying,' Malcolm said. 'Hey, I want a word with you, Jimbo. Come over here.' He led Jim away into a corner, leaving Agatha to get the coffees and carry them over. The age of chivalry is dead, she thought, but the age of equality has not yet dawned. What was that old song, 'Other People's Babies'? She sang it under her breath, paraphrased. 'Other people's husbands, that's my life, mistress to dozens, and nobody's wife.'

*   *   *

Lunch was unexpectedly successful. One thing that public school taught was social grace, and Gerry handled the business with an unselfconscious ease that Agatha found charming, especially after a morning of being one of the boys.

'I saw your father this morning,' she said to fill in a conversational pause. Gerry's face registered alarm.

'You didn't tell him—' he began explosively, and then stopped, confused.

'Tell him what?'

'Anything,' he said, looking down.

'Anything about what?' she insisted. Eventually he looked up, met her eye pleadingly.

'Well—only—I'd sooner he didn't know that I'd—that we'd—well, he'd make fun of me, you see. He's always making fun of me.'

'I don't suppose he means it—'

'I think he thinks it's funny. Only it's not. You won't tell him, Agatha, will you? Please.'

'All right,' she shrugged, and then to make him feel better, 'I don't suppose I'll see him again for months anyway. We don't often play together.'

'What was he doing there this morning?' Gerry asked.

'He said he needed the money.'

'For his mistress I suppose.' Agatha raised her eyebrows. 'Well, girl-friend, whatever you like to call her. It stands to reason if he's got to keep the house going and take her out and everything, he'd need extra money.'

Agatha regarded his blue-eyed youth questioningly. 'Does it upset you?'

'A bit,' he said. 'Not because of him, but because it upsets Mum. If she had a boy-friend it would be all right, but she feels left out.'

'That's very broadminded of you,' Agatha said. He shrugged. How exposed and vulnerable they were nowadays, she thought. In her childhood such things weren't to be contemplated, and therefore didn't happen. Now it seemed the norm—an abnormal norm, the balance of imbalance. How could such a fabric sustain them? The sail was rotten, and when a storm blew up it would simply shred. Then he cut through her thoughts with an innocent brutality.

'You were Dad's mistress once, weren't you?' Her mouth opened and shut. He went on, 'Oh I don't mind. I mean, no one ever found out about you, so it didn't count, did it?'

Fanelights again. Fingers crossed instead of legs crossed. 'How did you know?'

'I sort of guessed. Something about the way Dad talked about you when I started taking lessons from you. He was sort of startled when I told him your name.'

'I'll bet he was,' Agatha muttered. 'It was all over years ago,' she said, with what mad desire to justify herself she did not know. He shrugged again.

'I don't mind, really. It's nice—makes you a sort of second mother.'

'Hey,' she protested. 'Let's talk about something else. This is making me feel unnecessarily aged.'

After lunch they went outside on to the sunlit pavement, and Agatha stretched pleasantly. Wine and sunshine after a hard morning's work made her sleepy. 'Well,' she said. He lingered, looking at her. 'Where are you off to now?'

'Nowhere, really,' he said wistfully. 'Where are you?'

'I'm going home,' she said. 'I ought to have a bit of a blow this afternoon. I've got a tune on Friday. What are you going to do?'

'I haven't anything to do, particularly. Can I come home with you? I won't get in the way,' he said hastily to forestall her possible negative, 'only I don't want to go home just yet. Ma was in a state this morning.'

Oh Lord, Agatha thought, but he looked at her so appealingly that she could not refuse.

'All right,' she said, resigning herself. His face lit up, and he fell in beside her, almost but not quite taking her hand in his delight. 'You can carry my case for me,' she said, and he took that as a compliment too.

Fuck practice, she thought when they got home. It was hot and still, with that strange mid-afternoon pause about it, and she could not bring herself to shatter it with work or noise. She made a jug of lime with lots of ice, spread a blanket on the lawn, and stretched out on her back, her hands under her head, and he sat beside her and talked, and gradually, with the wine and the heat and not having slept much last night she fell asleep—

—and dreamed?

—and woke crying, crying out, something, what? and found herself in his arms, being held by him, stroked, while she whimpered and cried out—

—what?

'You were dreaming,' he said, trying to soothe her. 'It's all right now.'

The blackness receded, and the redness caused by sleeping in the sun, sun on her eyelids, the sun very bright outside and dark inside the—what?—inside the—barn?—and the sun bright outside and the dust falling through the sunlight in the doorway and he was standing there, very black against the sun—

'What was I saying?' she asked, dazed. He held her very tightly, stroking her head ineptly but with a hesitant tenderness.

'Nothing really, I don't know. You were crying. You said—'

'What?' she insisted.

'Nothing. You said let me be. That's all. You were just muttering.'

'I was dreaming,' she said dazedly, trying to look back through the curtain. But the images were receding, spinning away down the black vortex. She detached herself carefully from him and said more normally, 'Too much sun. I think I'll go in.'

'I'll come,' he said. He carried the blanket and the empty jug, out of the still hot garden into the cool dark house. The darkness dazzled her after the strong light outside.

'What's that smell?' she said, sniffing.

'It's lovely. I thought it was you,' he said. 'Your perfume.'

'No—it's—'

'I could smell it outside when you woke up. I thought it was you.'

'It's in here,' she said. 'The smell of apples.' She sniffed again. 'No, it's gone.' She shrugged. 'Let's go and listen to some music. Something undemanding. And then I'll make you an omelette or something. I'd better eat before I go out. Playing on an empty stomach isn't good for you. Put a record on, while I pop up to the loo.'

Afterwards she rinsed her face in cold water and washed her hands and then, to make her feel fresher, cleaned her teeth.

(Funny about the dentist's record card—)

Staring at her reflection as she scrubbed. Was it her imagination, or was there more blonde in her hair? Hard to say. Sunlight bleaching it? Crazy. Rinse and spit. Wipe. Better now. Hitch up tights—bloody things slipping down again. Must brown legs, do without them.

Back downstairs, and he had put on Brahms' Serenade. Okay. He sat on the sofa, and she sat on the floor, and he talked to her, and she looked at him, admiring him in a detached sort of way, his clear, pale, fair face, straight pale hair, beautiful blue eyes, young and unused. The child she had never had? But he was already born when she had had her affair with Jim. He had been four then, and Maggie had been expecting her second, the one she lost.

Two glorious years, and then guilt or habit or indolence or something had taken him back to Maggie, and there had followed ten years of distant, kindly friendship. Then, two years ago, when Phil had left her, and she had applied for licence to teach, Gerry had come to her. The Lord giveth, the Lord taketh away. But mostly taketh away.

Suddenly she became aware that all was not well. He was looking at her in a strange way—she thought he was going to be sick. What had he eaten at lunch? Some kind of fish, wasn't it? He was saying—

'—So beautiful, did you know that? Of course, you must—everyone must tell you so.'

'Gerry, for heaven's sake—' she began. 'Really, I'm not beautiful at all. You really must—'

'You are, you are. I've thought it for so long, and then today, when you were lying down, and I was just looking at you—' He drew a trembling breath. 'The sun was shining in your eyes, and they were just like butterfly's wings under glass, all iridescent, greeny blue, and those little dark flecks—'

'I have not got dark flecks in my eyes,' she said firmly, 'and besides—'

'Besides what?' he said, smiling at her. Good question. Behind her the music came to a stop at the end of the first movement, and the between-movements pause seemed to extend itself unnaturally into a silence that was not silence. The hair on the nape of her neck rose and she shivered involuntarily; the suspended moment was filled with the blue of his eyes and the smell of apples—

—the smell of apples dark inside the—barn?—bright outside he was cut out dark and sharp against the sunlight outside dark inside but not the boy no the boy and the smell of apples not the boy it was *him*—

But that was a dream.

'Why am I so afraid?' she said. 'Gerry, why am I so afraid?'

'I will help you,' he said, reaching out to her. 'Let me help you.'

'Oh God,' she said, and put her hands over her eyes.

CHAPTER THREE

On the whole she wasn't sorry when Polly arrived, although Polly was in a state, for it saved her from the full frontal force of Gerry's sympathy. Having introduced them one to the other she left them alone in the drawing-room while she escaped to the kitchen to cook omelettes, and when she returned in mid-exercise with a bottle of wine, a corkscrew and three glasses she found them both sitting on the floor deep in conversation.

'Here, one of you open this,' she said

briskly. 'I shall be about another ten minutes, so make yourselves comfortable.'

They looked up with a momentary blankness that showed they had forgotten her existence, and then Gerry shook himself. 'Oh, yes, all right. Shall I bring you a glass?'

'Don't bother. I'll catch up later. Don't forget I've got to work tonight.'

'Have you?' Polly said vaguely.

'Concert.'

'Oh.'

'Listen, Agatha, could I borrow your trumpet a minute? I want to show Polly something,' Gerry said eagerly. Agatha raised an eyebrow. 'I've got my own mouthpiece with me.'

'Well—' she hesitated. She didn't like anyone else using her instrument. 'Use my old one,' she said eventually. 'It's under the stairs. What do you want to show—oh, never mind,' as her nose brought her tidings from the kitchen. 'I must go—something's about to burn.'

She took her time in the kitchen, hearing voices, and then Gerry playing some ornaments, and then a fairly good imitation of a pibroch played on bagpipes, and laughter. That boy, she thought, has real talent. He even makes my old leaky job sound reasonable. If only—but then, life is full of if onlies. She carried the plates through, and switched on the lights as it was dim in the drawing-room once the sun had gone round.

'Oh, not too bright,' Polly objected. 'Can't you just have the lamps?'

She jumped up and rearranged the lighting to suit herself while Agatha put the plates and cutlery down on the floor and felt rather left out of things, for the atmosphere was so cosy between them. 'Help yourselves,' she said abruptly, and pulled out a coffee table for herself to eat from. Polly picked up a plate, and then came over to kiss the top of Agatha's head.

'Thanks,' she said. 'You're lovely. Hey, do you know, I think your hair's getting—'

'Worse?' Agatha finished for her drily. 'Thanks.'

'I wasn't going to say worse, but—more blonde, anyway. It really is strange, isn't it,' she said emphatically, pausing to think about it. Agatha looked up at her frown.

'Thanks again, for that really useful observation.'

Polly ignored the sarcasm. 'But what're you going to do about it, Ag?'

'There doesn't seem much I can do, does there?'

'I know, but—well, shouldn't you see someone about it? I mean, it might be—'

'Carry on.'

'Well, that's the trouble, isn't it? I mean there isn't anything it could be. But perhaps you should have a check-up or something?'

'The thought had occurred to me. Eat your omelette.'

'Really though. It might be something important.'

'All right,' Agatha said irritably. 'I will, as soon as I have time. Also, I mean to—'

'What?'

She hadn't meant to let so much out, but wearily she added, 'My eyes are playing me up. Perhaps while I'm at it I'll get them tested. I'm losing weight, too.'

Polly started at that, and looked anxiously into Agatha's face for a moment before turning away, embarrassed. Agatha knew why. Losing weight for no good reason was the dread symptom, wasn't it? The word that must never be breathed, lest you gave it power, like naming a demon. And couldn't that cause strange changes in the body too? Such as, perhaps, sudden bleaching of the hair? *Something hormonal*, or ladies' complaints, or any of the other acceptable euphemisms. Talk about sex, if you like, give a blow by blow account of last night's activities, but death and certain kinds of sickness were still taboo. Agatha ate broodingly, aware of a turbulent feeling inside her, like anger, but oddly disconnected; as if she had been inhabited by someone else's rage. The other two, after a glance or two at her preoccupied face, talked together quietly, like sickbed visitors.

Their conversation drifted the random way

of most such conversation, via the omelette and vegetarianism through the properties of herbs to the supernatural, magic and spiritualism.

'And of course it's Midsummer Eve today, isn't it,' Polly said, 'when spirits roam abroad. Just the time to contact the loved ones. Hey, have you read Evelyn Waugh?'

'We did *A Midsummer Night's Dream* for 'A' level,' Gerry said, a sentence behind.

'You're lucky,' Polly said. 'We did *A Winter's Tale*, and I still don't understand a word of it. All that about his dead daughter being turned into a statue and eaten by bears or something. And being raised by magic, whatever it was.'

'Why don't we have a go at the old Ouija board thing?' Gerry said eagerly, looking to Agatha for approval. 'We do it at school sometimes, it's fun. And tonight's the right night for it.'

'Yes, why not? Have you got a clean wine-glass, Ag? And the Scrabble letters?'

'They're no good, not big enough,' Gerry said quickly. 'At school we wrote the letters out on bits of card. We bought some postcards and cut them in half.'

'There's a pack of Lexicon cards in the dresser in the other room,' Agatha heard herself say.

'What're Lexicon cards?' Gerry asked vaguely, but Polly was already up and heading for the door. Agatha thought back to her own school days. It had been all the rage then, and apparently the fashion had arisen again at the same level. In the cramped and squalid prefects' room, five of them round a notched and battered table with a Lexicon pack and a wine glass brought from someone's home, in their free periods, after school, in the lunch hour, sometimes smoking illicit cigarettes, the height of their social naughtiness, sometimes entertaining prefects from the neighbouring boys' school over for joint theatrical endeavours. Agatha had had a strangely protracted and aimless friendship with the boy who played Sir Joseph Porter in the joint-schools *Pinafore*, and gained great kudos from it because he was, erroneously as it happened, believed to have *gone all the way* with an incredibly wicked girl in the upper fifth who was expelled for smoking a cigarette in the street outside the school after choir practice one Friday evening.

Nowadays, of course, they all knew about sex from the age of ten upwards, but then it was still the thing which was not spoken of, let alone done. That was before The Pill, before the entertainment value of sex had been successfully disconnected from its functional consequences, before the change had come over women, before freedom, liberation, talk of equality, if not the fact yet entirely, and smoking was the only socially acceptable naughtiness open to sixth-form girls from decent families. The smell of rotting apple-cores in the waste-paper-basket, and of spilt instant coffee, and of dust and chalk and books and plimsolls, and five earnest seekers after wisdom placing one aching forefinger on the upturned bottom of the glass and waiting for messages from the beyond which invariably turned out to be meaningless jumbles of letters. But oh the thrill when you felt the glass move under your finger, and the even greater thrill when it spelled a proper word!

'We do it at school a lot,' Gerry was saying, and taking over as the master of ceremonies he cleared the table Agatha had just finished eating from, and took the cards from Polly and began to sort out the alphabet. Agatha watched them, distantly amused, distantly disturbed.

'Trouble is,' Gerry said, 'none of us has got anyone who's died to contact, so probably we shan't get anything.'

'Agatha has,' Polly said. 'Haven't you, Ag? In fact, nothing but dead relatives.'

'I've told you a million times not to exaggerate. My mother and father, that's all.'

'That's all you know about,' Polly agreed. 'But for all you know you might have had uncles and aunts who were dead too. I mean, you certainly haven't any live ones, have you?'

Gerry looked interested. 'We could try for your mother,' he said. 'What was her name?'

'Agatha, of course,' Polly said. 'That's how

she got that name in the first place.'

'I think it's a lovely name,' Gerry said loyally. 'It means *the good*. Better than being called something that doesn't mean anything.'

'All right, get on with it,' Agatha said, trying to curb her irrational irritability. 'Never mind the semantics.'

'Now Ag, no racial prejudice. And no giggling, anyone. Nothing to disturb the vibes.'

Fingers on glass minutes of silence forearms aching self-consciousness fading to intent concentration tingling fingertips going dead and then *jerk* who did that? Eyes meet *not me* suspicion but then *jerk* again and at last the smooth slither, the slightly aching sound of the rim against the wooden table, slide and stop, waiting for a question.

'Say something,' Polly muttered to Gerry. Master of ceremonies, he straightened slightly and said,

'Is there anybody there?'

Slither, smooth, powerful, horrible at first, fingers stretching to go with it. 'Don't press so hard,' Agatha said to no one in particular. The glass scuffed before the Y card.

'Do you have a message for someone here?'

Y

'For which one of us?'

The glass surged and jerked on the spot. Agatha remembered those sessions at school, when each one had wanted it to spell her own name, and consciously or unconsciously urged it towards her own initial letter. It jerked again, and then skimmed off towards the W.

Meaningless jumble coming. Why am I doing this? Resigned. Amuse the children.

H. E. R. E.

'Where?' Gerry said puzzled, but it slithered on, gaining speed and strength as they went with it instead of trying to guide it.

ARE YOU

Their eyes met above the table. 'What's that supposed to mean?' Polly said. 'Who's pushing it?'

'Shush,' Gerry said. 'I'll ask the questions. Who are you?'

N

'Is there someone there? Have you a message?'

AGATHA.

They looked at her. She shrugged. 'You have a message for Agatha?'

'Are you Agatha's mother?' Polly asked, irrepressibly.

AGATHA.

'Shush, Polly, you're confusing it. Who are you?'

HE.

Agatha felt the hair rise on the nape of her neck again, and her eyes met Gerry's unwillingly. They were too blue, went on for too long. Don't ask any more, she pleaded, but even as she moistened her lips to say it he had said,

'What is your message?'

LET.

'No,' Agatha said. Polly looked up, curious. 'No more.'

ME.

'Stop it.' She took her finger away. It skimmed on unfalteringly.

IN. LET ME—

'Stop it!' She smacked at their hands, and they pulled back, startled, and alone, untouched, the glass slid on, gratingly, bumped the I card, and without a pause headed across the table for the N, almost reached it before Agatha with a blind sideswipe knocked it from the table. It rolled unbroken on its round side on the carpet and the three of them stared at it until it came to rest, half afraid it would get back on to the table of its own accord.

'Agatha, I'm sorry,' Gerry began. Polly reached out a hand and Agatha jumped up, tilting the table in her haste so that two cards planed off towards the floor.

'Don't touch me,' she cried. She was trembling, and astonished at herself because it was with rage, this strange, undirected rage. 'Leave me alone!'

'Ag, I'm sorry. It was only a joke,' Polly said inadequately. 'Don't get so upset. I shouldn't have—'

'You were pushing it?' Gerry said in disbelief. 'But—' Polly made a violent face at him, and Agatha pulled herself together with an effort.

'Never mind. Enough's enough. I'd better get this stuff cleared away. I'll have to be going soon.'

They helped her, subdued, and she made a further effort to revive her spirits and cheer them up.

'What are you doing tonight, you two?' she asked. 'Are you going out somewhere, Polly?'

'I haven't planned anything,' she said. 'I don't want to go home. I want to keep doing things. It's easier.'

Ah yes, she had forgotten for the moment the empty bed syndrome. 'Why don't you come to the concert? I'm pretty sure there should be seats left. Anyway, if there aren't, you can always watch from the side. You can hear well enough from there. If you've nothing else to do, anyway.'

Polly considered, and Gerry said, 'My dad will be there, won't he?'

'Mm. Does that make a difference?'

'Dunno. I suppose I ought to go and listen to him once in a while.'

'There won't be much to listen to. He's only bumping,' Agatha said.

'But if I went, you wouldn't—'

'Only if he asked. You wouldn't want me to lie, would you? But he won't ask. Why should he?'

'Would he like it, do you think?'

'Sure to. Everyone's flattered by attention.

Well, make your minds up. I'm going to have a quick wash, and then I'll have to be off.'

*   *   *

They came, and she got them seats in the front row, saw them into them, and then repaired to the brass players' dressing-room to have a blow. Malcolm was there, playing tunes, the only one of them who warmed up playing tunes, and mocked her as usual for her runs, scales and exercises. 'Bloody calisthenics' he called them. She called him Eddie Calvert, and honour was satisfied. 'Are you all right, though, Aggie?' he asked when he paused to shake the spit out of his valves. 'You're looking a bit knackered. Eyes still bothering you?'

She shrugged. 'I think I might be a bit under the weather. I've lost a bit of weight.'

'Never mind,' he said, pinching her. 'You're still cuddly enough.'

'What I mean is, without trying to. Perhaps I should see a doctor?' She said it wistfully, in the hopes that he would say either yes or no heartily enough to make her mind up for her, but Bill intervened.

'Aye, I should let doctor have a look at your chest. After all, you've let everyone else—why leave him out?'

'Ha ha,' she said witheringly. Bill smirked and blew a devastating raspberry on his trumpet and wandered away, but before

Agatha could resume Jim Blackburn burst in looking hot and bothered.

'I've just seen my brat sitting out front,' he said. 'Did you bring him, Ag?'

'Not exactly,' she began, but he put a wild hand through his hair, cutting her off.

'Bloody hell, that about sews it up. I wish to Christ you'd told me. That really puts the—can't you put him off or something?'

'What's the matter, Jimbo? Can't stand the competition? I hear that lad of yours is going to be good.'

'Oh shut it, Malcolm. The point is Diana's here, and she'll be coming back in the interval, and if the two of them meet—'

'Oh,' Malcolm said, turning away indifferently. He had no time for other people's marital problems. 'Well, it was bound to happen some time, wasn't it?'

'Tell him not to come back, will you?' Jim said to Agatha. She shrugged.

'If you like. But it won't guarantee he won't. In fact rather the reverse. But surely he won't make a fuss?'

'If you think that, then you don't know Gerry. I don't know where he gets his puritan streak—well, I do, of course, it's from Maggie and her bloody Calvinist up-bringing. Oh lor'.'

'Can't you tell Diana not to come back?'

'Too late now. I'll just have to try and intercept her when we come off. But I wish you hadn't interfered, Agatha, really I do.'

It was said mildly enough, but the suppressed and bubbling spring of new anger in her was released by it, and surged up into the light. She didn't know quite what she said to him, but it was said loudly and vehemently enough to bring Malcolm back in with the chairman behind him. 'Will you f'fucksake shut up you two? We could hear you right down the passage. And come on—we're on now. Didn't you hear the bell?' He turned on his heel, muttering, 'Bloody women—always the same when you let bloody women in. Never had this trouble in the old days.'

And Agatha, to her own astonishment as much as anyone's, lashed out at him, hitting him clumsily and ludicrously on the shoulder. He stopped and turned, and for a moment they were all frozen in tableau, staring at each other in fear and embarrassment at something having been let loose. Malcolm's face suffused with blood, became dangerously dark, and for a moment as she saw his fist close up Agatha knew with a horrible certainty that he was going to hit her, and that it was going to hurt badly. And then she started to black out. Her knees buckled, and it was only Malcolm's quick reaction that caught her before she fell. 'What the fuck's wrong with you anyway, Aggie?' he muttered. 'You've changed, girl, y'know that?'

'I'm sorry, it was my fault,' Jim said belatedly. 'I upset her.'

'She's bloody easy to upset, that's all I know. What's up with you? It's too early for the change, isn't it?' He regarded her a moment longer, took in the misery in her expression, and recalled himself to his duty. 'Oh, forget it,' he said, his voice reaching for normality. 'Come on, we've got work to do. Come on, pal, forget it. Let's get out there and give 'em hell.' He put a kindly arm round her shoulder, gave her a little comforting squeeze, knowing full well that being upset gives rise to lousy performances, and then took his arm away with an involuntary start. 'Bloody 'ell, you have lost some weight. You feel like a pound of soup bones.'

Auto-pilot again. They went on, they played, they stood for applause, they came off. Agatha went to get herself a drink, and Malcolm found her and said, 'I think you'd better go home and get some sleep. You look like hell. Mike says he'll play the second half for you. Go on home and get an early night, and go and see the doctor tomorrow. Right?'

He wasn't giving her the option. She was dismissed, and the warning was there implicitly—sort yourself out, or you've had it. If she was once thrown out of the orchestra she would be finished, she'd never get another job; but there was no arguing with Malcolm, who was head of the section and on the board and a very influential man in his own right. All she said was, 'I played all right, didn't I?'

'Yeah. You were all right, girl. Don't worry. Just get an early night.' She searched his face for sincerity, but his eye was as flat as the sole of a boot, and she could only obey without comment or fuss. She packed up her hooter, changed out of her long skirt into her trousers, and went out through the fire exit to avoid having to face anyone.

That was how she came to miss the terrible row between Jim and Gerry over Diana, which ended with Jim throwing Gerry metaphorically out of the paternal home, and Gerry going off and getting extremely drunk, and arriving on her doorstep just before midnight looking for a night's lodging with options on the next few weeks. Agatha was not amused, and though out of pity she took him in, she did not quite see how he could have done anything less convenient for her if he had thought about it with both hands for a month, because when he rang her doorbell she was in bed with Joe, and when she let Gerry in he talked in a loud and drunken voice about having no one but her left, darling Agatha, which Joe had no difficulty in taking exception to.

'Oh, for God's sake,' Agatha said to them both impartially, and,

'I'll ring you some time,' said Joe, leaving.

CHAPTER FOUR

Two days down in Bristol doing Belshazzar's Feast, playing in the stage band. It was restful, and something of an Old Boys' Reunion of all the freelancers she hadn't seen for ages. An ambitious programme for a provincial festival, and it went well despite its quota of accidents. In the first section the orchestra leader during a five-bar rest dropped his bow over the edge of the platform and had to have it retrieved by a member of the audience; five minutes later the conductor, bringing his baton down emphatically, snapped it in half against his music stand with a noise that rivalled the fabled Festival Hall 65-Decibel Cough. Then one of the violas came in spare and the second clarinet dropped his mouthpiece and split the reed. And then half way through the last section Agatha became aware that her period had come on.

As soon as they came off she hastened to the loo to make adjustments. She caught it in time, and sat for a moment contemplating the event with the usual mixture of relief and exasperation. Relief that she was apparently functioning correctly, despite recent health worries, and exasperation that the lunar nuisance had turned up again. So much of life spent menstruating, until the time came when it stopped and one spent the rest of life mourning its passing. Half the female population of the country in terror of being pregnant and the other half in despair of being infertile. No wonder Romances ignored it all, postulated the ideal world where the female anguish of the Curse and the male anguish of Not Being Able to Get it Up never intruded. She fantasized pleasantly about a romantic novel where the heroine, dressed in white silk and dining with the square-jawed type she was always arguing with to disguise the fact that she was in love with him, suddenly came on and found herself unable to get up from the table for fear of revealing the wet brown stain on the back of her skirt. Oh yeah?

Someone had written along the bottom of the toilet door 'Beware of Limbo Dancers' and another hand, larger and bolder, had written along the top of the door 'Beware of Irish Limbo Dancers'. A distinct improvement on the usual standard of graffiti. Why was it that the scrawl in women's bogs was always more obscene and less witty than in men's? Even at University, such all-time greats as 'Take Heart—the Pope is 80% Water' and 'The Swan won't go in the Fridge' had been interspersed with crude drawings of giant penises like primitive moon-rockets.

Safe in here. Sometimes in the loo she would get a moment's panic that there was a concealed camera-eye somewhere and someone was filming her in this most vulnerable of positions. But on the whole, it was the one place you could be entirely yourself, entirely safe, entirely honest. Except that your thoughts followed you in, and spoke out loud and clear from the sudden silence in your mind. *Her clothes were all too big for her.* Sometimes when being cuddled by Phil she had received like a transmission from his mind the impression of what her body felt like to his arms, small and encircleable, narrow and flexible. She had now like a subliminal flash the impression of her body, little and compacted inside her clothes, as if it was shrinking, shrinking. Suppose, like Alice, she went on getting smaller and smaller, closing up like a folding telescope; suppose she winked out altogether, leaving her clothing like an empty snake-skin, like a sucked-out husk of a fly on a spider's web?

One pain drives off another. Think about something worse, to take your mind off it. All right, think about the future, about what life holds, about growing old, about dying without having achieved anything, dying alone and lonely, probably partly disabled, unable to keep clean, incontinent, dying alone of the cold in a bed in a smelly damp room, and thinking what did I live for? How about the rest of your life, pointless, fruitless, directionless, lonely, lonely, lonely?

Ah yes, that was better. That was really something to go out and get drunk to forget about. She braced up, laced up, flushed and departed. Outside Malcolm was hovering.

'Come on, Aggie. Masturbation is the thief of time, you know. We're going down the nearest filling station. Y' coming?'

'That's the most intelligent thing you've said this year,' she said, falling in with him. A glance at his face told her he was in mental gestation, and when they went through the swing doors and on to the fire-staircase he gave birth with some apparent anguish.

'I hear tell,' he said trying to sound diffident, 'that you've got Jim Blackburn's nipper.'

'Depends what you mean by got.'

'Well, word is, you're like up to no good.'

'Word is, he's up me? I don't know how these things get about, really I don't.'

'Bit much, isn't it, Aggo?'

'What, the way things get about?'

'No, I mean—well, Jimbo's going to be very cut up about it. Especially since you and him—well, it makes it a bit like incest, dunt it?'

'Oh for Chrissakes, Malcolm. It isn't true. The boy's stopping with me, that's all. What do you take me for?'

'No, honestly, I'm very relieved to hear it. I didn't believe a word of it anyway.'

'Well, don't put it about, will you?'

'Me? Talk? Silent-as-the-grave job, me. C'mon, I'll buy you a pint.'

Curse, Agatha thought, it'll be all over London in twenty-four hours that I've got the boy tied to the bed by the elastic out of his Y-fronts; and every single person will be convinced they never breathed a word to anyone. The amazing thing was how little ever got outside the magic circle. Everyone in the trade knew everything about everyone in the trade, but around them all was a kind of force-field that held outsiders outside.

'Y'know,' he said casually as they homed in on the lights of a pub, 'I'm quite getting used to you being blonde. It very nearly suits you.' Push doors, gust of warm smoky air carrying conversation like bacteria and the smell of convention, the element they lived in. No time to wonder until later quite what he meant by the 'nearly'; or how he knew about the boy in the first place.

* * *

Phone.

'Where've you been?'

'Bristol, actually. Not that that really counts as a where. What's up, Polly?'

'Oh darling, something absolutely wonderful's happened.'

'What's his name?' Sigh.

'What do you mean, what's his name? Why should it be a man?'

'Isn't it always?'

'Yeah. Well, I suppose nearly always. Oh but Ag, this one's lovely. I was working late, y'see, and we all went for a drink afterwards in the Cheshire Cheese, and this fabulous bloke turned up—a friend of Costos's actually, works for the *Telegraph* but don't hold that against him—and honestly, I could hardly breathe. You know what I mean—you know men like that?'

'Yes.' Phil, when she first met him, before marriage made him dull; and even longer ago, Jim Blackburn had had that power to turn your bones to water. Gerry had a little of it—perhaps in six or seven years time, he would be just such a killer.

'Well, we were all just chattering amongst ourselves, you know, and I could just *feel* his eyes on me. You know how you know when they're interested? Anyway, when closing time came he was sort of standing there looking spare, so I went up to him and said could I give him a lift anywhere, and he said he lived in Wimbledon and could I drop him at a tube. So I gave him a lift, and we were talking as we drove along, and then he just said, right out of the blue, "Would you prefer to go to your house or mine?"'

A long silence and warm breath as Polly relived the moment and Agatha smiled in recollection. Perhaps the best moment of an affair was that one when you knew you were going to go to bed with him: that lovely mixture of satisfaction and anticipation. After that, it was all downhill, slope it how you like.

'And which did you?'

'His. I'd a fancy to see it. It's a lovely house, and, oh Ag, he's got *the* most perfect taste. I was terrified it was all going to turn out to be Habitat and *Sunday Times Magazine*, but you know if I'd done it myself I think it would have looked just like that.'

'And what was his bed like?'

'Big and hard,' she said, and laughed. 'No, that was terrific too. I mean really wow-too-much time, y'know?'

Agatha braced herself for the last, first question. 'And is he married?'

'No-o,' Polly said, but the hesitation gave her away.

'What's the snag?'

'Well, he was married and he's now divorced, and they get on well and that's no problem. But he's had this girlfriend for about two years.'

'Oh *Polly*!'

'No, honestly, it's all right. She doesn't live with him or anything. He was quite open about it.'

'Pol, you *know* what's going to happen.'

'No, Ag, it's different this time. He really is smitten, you know. I mean, it isn't just—it's different. He was really—oh, you know, passionate and caring and—'

'—and when are you going to see him next?'

'Tonight.' Long sweet sigh. 'It'll be all right this time.'

Putting the phone down a little later,

Agatha thought bitterly, 'Oh darling, one always thinks that—every, every time.'

She gave Gerry his lesson—at least she didn't have to travel far for it now—and told him about it.

'And Wimbledon, of all places.'

'It isn't far,' Gerry said reasonably.

'But it's south of the river,' she said, and he grinned.

'I once lived in Richmond,' he said.

'Well, there you are, you see. You ought to know how Londoners regard the river. We tend to divide the capital into cis-pontine and trans-pontine London, and practically start looking out the elephants at the mention of crossing. Talking of which, have you called up your parents yet?'

Gerry's handsome young face grew sulky. 'Pa phoned me up while you were out, but we only yelled at each other. I think Ma's giving him hell, and he has to take it out on someone.'

'And what did you say to him?'

'He seemed to think—' he began and stopped abruptly.

'What?' Agatha said wearily. 'Oh I know—that you and I were—'

'Well, yes. I suppose it's natural.'

'It's bloody unnatural,' she said crossly. 'And what did you tell him?'

He looked uncomfortable.

'You let him go on thinking—'

'Well—'

'Oh Gerry!'

'Well what would you have done in my place?' he asked, cheeks reddening. She sighed and turned away. When it was a choice between her reputation and his pride, was it realistic to expect any man to sacrifice the latter?

* * *

A clear night, with the most wonderful moon, sailing brilliant and clear like a white-hot sixpence and flooding the street with such an intense blue-silver light that it quite negated the orange street-lighting. She left the curtains back and moved her head on the pillow so that her face was bathed in it, as if it had some healing property, and slept.

When she woke, the moonlight was off her face and lying in a long stripe down the side of the bed, and she wondered hazily if she ought to be able to deduce what the time was from that when she became aware that she was not alone in the bedroom. Her head whipped round on the pillow, and she saw that He was there, standing beside the bed, on the dark side; so she mustn't have woken, she must still be asleep, for this was the dream, wasn't it?

He bent forward towards her, and in the passive languor of her sleeping state she lay still and watched him. He eased the bedclothes back, drawing them down her body, and she felt the cool air touching her bare skin. Realistic. And then his hands gently caressing her. They were wonderfully smooth, almost unnaturally smooth, silky-skinned and cool, as if he had never used them for work in his life. They ran lightly down her sides to her waist and then up to her breasts, cupping over them, drawing the nipples upwards between finger and thumb, tugging them gently; and as they stiffened under the touch she saw his mouth curve into a smile.

Hands still on her breasts, he sat down on the edge of the bed, and she saw in the reflected glow of the moonlight that he was as naked as she. A small man, with powerful, rounded shoulders, and fair hair, and a clean-shaven face so full of shadows that it was impossible to see his features, although she knew it was the same man, knew she would recognize him if ever she saw him in daylight. And she felt his touch quite distinctly, felt a quiver of sensual enjoyment run through her as he dipped his head and closed his mouth around one of the nipples that he held up ready between his fingers.

His mouth was moist and silky and strangely cool. He certainly knew what to do. With his right hand holding her left breast up and forward, he sucked lustily, and she felt her womb contract sharply with that exotic, dangerous delight, and she gave a little gasping groan of pleasure. As if at that signal, his other hand left her breast and began to slide smoothly down over her waist and hip, and she relaxed her legs in anticipation.

And it was then that she looked down at his head, bent over her as he suckled; she saw his hair, the exact texture of it, the individual hairs, the curve of their spring from the scalp glittering slightly in the blueish light, and the upper edge of his ear and its delicate scroll-work. Dreams were often realistic, but they never had that kind of detail.

'This is not a dream,' she said aloud, and at the sound of her own voice, she knew she was awake, and horror swept over her. 'No!' she cried out, struggling away from his mouth, struggling to sit up. She put her hands against his shoulders, feeling for a fraction of a second under her panic that the flesh (it was flesh) warmed at her touch, and tried to push him away.

'Let me be.' It was a whisper, presumably from him; but at the same moment she began to scream, and at once the resistance of real flesh and bone against her hands was gone, he was in some mysterious way distant at the foot of the bed without any transition, and as she screamed again, wildly, she knew she was alone in the room, though she did not see him vanish, though there was no time between not being alone and being alone, as if they were the same thing, and she was still struggling to sit up when the door burst open and Gerry dashed in, snapping on the light as he came.

'What is it? What's happened?' he was babbling. She was still shrieking almost automatically, and she could hear her own voice, and see her own naked arms reaching out in terror for comfort even while another part of her was quite cool and collected, calm enough to observe that Gerry was wearing the bottoms of a pair of striped pyjamas and his hair was ruffled upwards so that it looked as if it was standing on end with fright. Her arms reached him and she felt the safe reassuring hard warmth of a real human being's back against her hands and his bare, hairless chest against her face.

Automatically he put his arms round her and stroked her hair and said,

'There, there, it's all right. What was it, a nightmare?'

Her incoherent stream of words slowed and clarified. She was sobbing for breath, and she could feel her own heartbeat thundering away unnaturally against his chest, but she was able to say,

'I dreamed—the man was here—by the bed—again—touching me.'

Her heartbeat slowed. Gerry sat on the edge of the bed, still holding her against him, and his hand soothing her head grew less sure as she grew more calm and their normal statuses were restored. She knew as if she could read his mind the exact moment he became painfully aware that she was naked and that her breasts were against his bare skin.

'If you're all right—I'd better—' he began to mutter. She didn't want him to go.

'Wait,' she said, gently detaching herself. She kept a nightie under her pillow in case she got cold in the night. While he averted his head in embarrassment, she fished for it and pulled it on and restored normality.

'You let out such a terrible shriek, I thought you were being murdered,' he said, trying to lighten the atmosphere with a joke.

'Then it was very brave of you to run in like that,' she said. She told him about the dream (dream?) or at least that she had thought the man was sitting on the bed touching her.

'A recurrent nightmare?' she wondered aloud. 'Except that it isn't like a nightmare. He doesn't seem evil.'

'Then why is it so frightening?' Gerry asked. With his hair standing on end he looked nearer fourteen than eighteen. In this particular striping of light and shadow she could see how the muscles of his lips were developing, pushing his upper lip down and inwards so that the pink everted part was beginning to disappear. She would be rather sorry when the process was complete—playing the trumpet spoiled their beauty, of course. Still, better that than those horrible scars fiddle players got, or the ugly stubby fingers of cellists—

'I suppose because it isn't natural. And then—he wants something. The dream—is sort of cumulative. Next time, perhaps he'll get further. And then what? I'm afraid—' She remembered—'He said "Let me be."'

'That's a funny thing to say, when it's him should be letting *you* be,' Gerry said. She frowned.

'I think he—'

'Hm?'

She shook her head. 'I don't know. Something was on the tip of my mind but—'

'Look,' he began. He was looking awkward, and she knew at once what he was going to say, and was grateful. 'Look, if you keep having this dream—well—do you think it might be better for you if you had some company? I mean,' he rushed on now, 'if I were to sleep in here with you—just sleep I mean—perhaps you wouldn't have the dream. Or if you started to dream it, you could call me, and I'd wake up, and it would go away. What do you think?'

She smiled at him. 'You are kind,' she said, and meant it. 'I was going to suggest it myself.'

He looked uncertainly at her. He evidently had not thought ahead as far as her acceptance of his offer. 'Well, shall I get my bedclothes? And sleep on the floor?'

She hid her broadening smile. 'No, come in with me. It's a good big bed, and I know I can trust you to behave. I'd be glad of the company.'

His confusion was complete. He made to go round the bed, but she stopped him with, 'You'd better turn off the light first.'

'Oh yes—sorry.'

He padded over to the door, snapped the switch, and disappeared into the dark. She heard his breathing and his soft heavy body moving slowly back across the room, groping uncertainly, afraid of bumping into something. She felt his knees contact the bottom of the bed, felt him grope round the foot of it with his hands, and then the creak and tilt of the mattress as his weight came on to the edge of it (it had not tilted when He sat down) and the puff of cooler air as he lifted the clothes to get under. He lay down, on his back, on the far side of the bed, rigid with care not to touch her, and she sighed and relaxed ostentatiously and turned over on her side. She really was grateful for his presence; not because he could stop her dreaming, but at least his presence would make it possible for her to tell when she was dreaming and when awake. That was the really frightening part about it all.

She lay awake for a long time, listening to the child's breathing growing steadier and lighter, feeling by some process of sympathy when he relaxed and when he fell asleep. She began to doze lightly. The moonlight slid out of the room, and Gerry turned over in his sleep and coming up against her dropped an arm lightly across her and rested his head against her shoulder. She smiled and slept.

CHAPTER FIVE

'I don't know what's wrong with men nowadays,' Polly said gloomily as they shuffled along the salad bar serving themselves. 'What on earth's that? Yeuch. It looks like vomit.'

'Dunno. I think it might be marrow, chunks of marrow in salad cream.'

'Fuck me, what will they think of next,' she said more mildly and took a spoonful. 'Come to think of it, they all look pretty much like—'

'Remember Barry McKenzie on the cross-channel ferry? "Jeez, I don't remember eating that"? Sweet-corn and tomato skins.'

'Yes, thank you very much, we'll let you know,' Polly said, taking a spoonful of rice mixture.

'I think the emancipation of women came as a shock to their psyches,' Agatha said, sticking to lettuce and green peppers.

'Who?'

'Men.'

'But that was years ago. They should be used to it by now.'

'You're fooling yourself, duckie. It happened last year if it happened at all.'

They queued and paid and went back to their table. It was one of those self-consciously ethnic wine-bars with sawdust on the floor and messages chalked on blackboards about the day's special and end-of-bin bargains, but the house wine was a very good blanc-de-blanc and the salad was reasonably cheap.

'I think you're right,' Polly said through a mouthful of possibly-marrow. 'Have you noticed how often the poor blighter, after a perfectly divine screw, will apologize for not having gone on longer?'

Agatha nodded sadly. 'It's the Olympic complex. They will read these tit magazines with those yawn-making "True Confessions" from self-styled studs. There's so much talk about sex nowadays that they're all terrified of not measuring up.'

'Whereas the worst thing you can do is apologize. I mean, there one is, absolute bliss, flat out and panting, think whee! and the next thing this little voice in the ear says "I'm sorry but I just couldn't hold on any longer" as if he's wet the bed or something. Who wants him to hold out longer? Personally, I'd rather they were so overcome with lust for me—there's something positively insulting about all that self-control. But they will harp on about the time-limit, poor buggers.'

'It sounds as if you've been having trouble with your new creature—hey, I don't even know his name. Has he got one, or is it just darling?'

'Don't be smart, you old bucket, of course

he's got a name.' Polly went on eating. Agatha eyed her speculatively.

'Well?'

'Well what?'

'What is his name?'

'Oh, didn't I tell you?' Polly said innocently.

'No, you didn't. What's wrong? I know, it's something dreadful.'

'It isn't,' Polly said, reddening. 'Well, lots of people are called it. It could be a lot worse. Well, it could be worse anyway.'

'Not Trevor?' Agatha breathed in awe. Polly looked down at her plate and carefully drew the rind off a piece of garlic sausage.

'It's Brian, actually,' she said, aiming at casualness. Agatha choked and buried her face in her napkin, and Polly watched her stonily. 'All right,' she said at last, 'it isn't that bad. Anyway,' a wicked smile began to creep up one corner of her mouth, 'I haven't told you the name of his other girl-friend yet.' She watched Agatha's recovery, timing the next stroke. 'It's Janice.'

'Woop!' This time they were both off. Agatha surfaced first. 'Ey, it's good to 'ave a laff occasionally,' she sighed, wiping her eyes. 'Oh Pol, you really can't fall seriously in love with a man called Brian.'

'It has been done.'

'I don't believe it. Produce the evidence.'

'Oh well—but we're having a lovely time together. And it's really—I mean he's really—

well—'

'All right, then what's the problem?'

Polly sighed. 'I just don't know where I am with him,' she said. Agatha heard the words of doom. For herself, she had fallen in love three times since Phil left her, and each time had discovered the same thing, that she just didn't know where she was with them.

'Blows hot and cold?' she hazarded. Polly nodded, as if she had admitted something shameful.

'We went out for a meal last night, in this really nice place at Camden Lock—do you know it?'

'Not Le Routier?'

'Yeah. You been there?'

'George used to take me there,' Agatha said, naming a seed that had fallen on stony ground some months back.

'Oh well, you know it then. We had a super meal, and lots of wine, and admittedly we were both a bit pissed, but not that badly. And we went home, and he was really loving, and he was talking about the future, and making plans for it, you know, things like where were we going to live, and where should we have our holidays, just as if we were going to get married—'

'Did he mention marriage?'

'Not the actual word.' Polly paused, put off her stroke. 'And we had the most marvellous screw, best ever, and fell asleep, and you know it was one of those nights when you keep waking up and doing it again. And then this morning he was as cool as he's ever been, and saying he didn't know whether he could see me this weekend and he couldn't give up Janice and all that sort of thing. I just wanted to scream.'

Polly shovelled down the last of her vomit salad and made a face over it as if it tasted as bad as it looked. Agatha stared at her with sympathy, wondering how long it would take her to realize how hopeless it was. If he was as equivocal as that—

'I wonder why one never meets anyone uncomplicated? Listen, if you ever meet a decent bloke who isn't attached, and wants to be, let me know and we'll throw a party on the strength of it.'

'I know what you mean. But there's Gerry for you at least.'

'There isn't, for Chrissakes. He's half my age. It isn't like that, and I wish you'd get it into his head.'

'Don't you mean my head?'

'I know what I mean. But seriously, Pol, you know what this blighter's doing to you. He just wants the best of both worlds, and you're encouraging him. Why should he give either of you up when he can have both?'

'It isn't like that. You don't understand,' Polly said. Agatha heard the hint of irritability and backed off. At this stage of an affair one always wanted to believe it was different, and as every con-man knows, the art is telling the lie the mark wants to believe.

'Have you heard any more from Joe?' Polly asked after a moment. It was an obvious warning buoy, and Agatha took it up.

'No. I don't suppose I will now. I think he was probably getting bored anyway, and was glad of the excuse.'

'Poor Ag.'

'Oh, I don't mind. It wasn't a big thing.'

'From what I heard, it was a very big thing.'

'Rude!' Agatha grinned. 'But you know what I mean. I shall miss him in bed. He was so marvellously uncomplicated about sex. He did it, and enjoyed it, and that was that. I should think he's probably the only man I've ever bedded with who didn't underneath it all despise me for going to bed with him.'

'Oh, come on, Ag, it isn't like that any more.'

'Not on the surface, but underneath, you know, they still think it's different for men and for women. They get very cross if you won't, but if you will it proves you're not a nice girl. But EW at least didn't have those hang-ups. And he never apologized for a performance in his life.'

'Never mind the length, feel the quality,' Polly said. 'I don't know where they get the idea they have to go on for hours.'

'I told you, it's those ghastly magazines, full

of pictures of women with blurred fannies.'

Polly giggled. 'Isn't it terrible when they say "I'm not going to come until you've come again" and all you want is to go to sleep. And they go on and on and on—'

'And in the end you have to fake it or they'd never stop. So you start the heavy breathing and the groaning—'

'And then, if you get the timing wrong and they don't come, you've got to go through the whole business again. It's terrible lying there trying to pace them and getting sorer and sorer and getting cramps in your legs—'

'And your hair getting all sweaty when you only washed it that morning and you know you daren't wash it again for another day or it'll go limp and greasy. Oh the things one thinks of. It's all so different in real life from the magazines, isn't it? None of this fireworks and fountains and shooting stars business. Just the way no one in fiction ever suffers from diarrhoea.'

A pause. Polly studied her friend. 'You know,' she said at last, 'I've got so used to seeing you blonde I hardly notice it any more. It shows you how quickly one adjusts. Did you ever try to find out what caused it?'

Agatha had been looking for something in her handbag down by her feet but now she looked up quickly, and Polly saw the flash of fear in her freckled eyes. Strange how those dark flecks showed up more in this light. She'd hardly noticed them before.

'No, I didn't. I've been busy. I—' Agatha noticed her hands trembling and clasped them together on the table. 'I've had so much to do, and I haven't been sleeping well recently. I don't suppose it's important.' Not as important as—

'Well, thousands of women spend a fortune trying to go that colour, so I suppose you're lucky. You haven't been holding out on us, and secretly dying it all along, have you?'

'Nah, course not. Come on, let's go. This place is getting stuffy.'

'All right. Where's your horn?'

'S'all right, I've got it. All right?'

They gathered their possessions and slipped through the crowded tables to the door. In the street Polly went to put an arm across Agatha's shoulder and misjudged the distance badly. She was about to say something like 'Are you standing down a hole or something?' but checked herself in time. Her friend, she observed, was standing on the level pavement, and wearing moderate sized heels, yet Polly could put her arm round her shoulders without lifting it. They used to be of a height. Now Agatha was definitely shorter. A cold breath of fear touched her too. Some change was coming over Agatha, and Agatha knew it and was afraid.

'Ag, have you ever thought—' Agatha looked up at her, and there was as much pleading as fear in her eyes. Not yet, then—but something must be done. Polly wondered how much influence Gerry had over her. Did they really not screw? She would have a word with him, try to get him to persuade Ag to go to the doctor. She turned her friend in the direction of the street where the car was parked. 'I think I'd like to go to Boulogne, just for the day, sometime. Have you thought of that?' she said, steering the conversation to safety; Agatha, knowing full well what Polly was thinking, allowed it to be steered.

* * *

It was hot and Agatha was restless, could not sleep. She was afraid of dreaming. At last she got up the will to rise. I'll have a wash, cool myself down, and a drink of something, and then try again. She padded through the silent house to the bathroom and put the light on. She had to wait a few minutes for her eyes to adjust, and then she ran tepid water into the basin and pressed her flannel, which had dried out rigid as usual, into it, and began slowly to rinse her face and neck and upper body.

She stared at her reflection in the mirror over the sink; absently, not really seeing it; and then slowly the realization dawned on her that she was looking up at it; rising slightly on to her toes to do so. The mirror was too high for her.

But she had fixed it herself, after Phil had gone, for doing her make-up. Had Gerry moved it, for his own shaving purposes? But no, she had seen him this morning bending his knees at it—and besides, it was fixed with grab tabs, and you could see—she went on tiptoe and peered at the wall—that there were no other marks on the wall. Besides, some inner awareness of proportion told her that the distance between the top of the mirror and the ceiling was unchanged. It was a low ceiling this side, the roof sloping down here, and when Phil had the mirror up for his height there had only been a gap of about three inches above.

Her mind shied away from the conclusion, and her stomach swooped sickeningly as she hauled it back.

You're getting smaller. Aren't you? Aren't you?

Clothes too big, trousers too long, not because you're losing weight. You're a size smaller. Maybe two sizes. *You're shrinking*.

Which is impossible.

She looked at her face, paper white in the bright bathroom light, framed with blonde hair (blonde hair! Dear God!) looked into her own frightened eyes, blue eyes, she had always had rather attractive blue eyes, blue eyes with brown flecks, there had never been brown flecks before but now there were brown flecks in her blue eyes and they were getting bigger weren't they all the time more brown and less blue they were changing too weren't they like the hair going blonde she was changing into a brown-eyed blonde wasn't she eyes and hair changing colour—

Which is impossible.

Oh Lord God what's happening to me? Shall I die? I don't want to die. I'm so afraid

(Go to the doctor)

that I will die. Something horrible happening inside me something hormonal or even the Big C can't even say the word in my head too terrible but I don't want to die I am afraid

(Go to the doctor)

but I'm healthy aren't I I function all right except that I'm very tired these days but that's understandable lots of work and not sleeping well and I never sleep well in the summer and the heat is trying but basically I'm healthy I can't go to the doctor and say I'm perfectly healthy and everything but I'm changing

Which is impossible.

She let the water out of the basin and stood shivering, looking at the black window and not seeing it. Inside her mind she said very quietly, help me, oh help me. Her shivering stopped, and after a long moment she turned and walked, slowly but with purpose, out of the bathroom, turning off the light, and then, in the dark, downstairs and into the dining-room. She went to the dresser and opened the drawer and took out the pack of Lexicon cards, and reached up into the top of the dresser and drew out a wine glass. The dining-room table was clear and she put the glass down, stem-up, in the centre of it. The Lexicon pack hadn't been shuffled and the alphabet was on the top, in order. She dealt them slowly round in a circle and then for another long moment stood staring at the arrangement as if in hesitation. The moon was waning and was round the back of the house so it was almost dark in the room, but the white cards with their black letters stood out clearly enough against the dark wood of the table. Very slowly she reached out and placed her forefinger on the foot of the glass.

Nothing happened. She relaxed with sudden relief. She did not know whether she had expected nothing or something, but it was a relief that nothing had happened. She stared at the glass, feeling foolish, but oddly triumphant. So much for your power, she thought. Where are you now?

And then the glass moved.

Her heart stopped momentarily with sheer terror because she wasn't pushing it, it was moving away from her finger, on its own. She pulled her hand back and it stopped. Her eyes wide with apprehension, she reached out again and touched it. At once it jerked away, as if impatiently, as if it had been waiting for her to turn it on. She let her finger go with it, and it ran smoothly, as if on casters, to the A, bumped it impatiently and went sideways towards the G.

AGATHA AGATHA.

'Who are you?' she whispered.

AT LAST.

'Who are you?' she whispered.

YOUR OWN.

What do you want? She did not whisper it aloud, she merely thought it, but the answer came, drawing her hand back and forth across the table as the glass skimmed.

LET ME BE.

How can I let you be? It is you must let me be.

I CANNOT BE WITHOUT YOU. YOU MUST LET ME IN.

'No!' she whispered, but she did not pull her hand away. The glass moved on. She became aware that it made no sound, the light grating sound it had made before when the three of them did it was missing, as if it were not touching the table at all.

I HAVE WAITED FOR YOU SO LONG.

Who are you?

YOU KNOW WHO I AM. YOU AND I HAVE ALWAYS BEEN. I NEED YOU. YOU MUST LET ME IN.

I don't want to. I am afraid.

LOVE ME. LOVE ME. LOVE ME.

She pulled her hand away, and held it with the other as if it might be snatched back without her volition. The glass slid to a halt, and she stared at it, almost feeling that it was staring back at her; pleading or demanding?

'Who are you?' she said again. In the silence of her head she heard the words 'You know who I am'. It was true and not true, in the same way that she recognised the face of the man who stood beside her bed, and yet did not know him. The knowledge was just outside her grasp, but within reach. Moving nearer? She did not want to know. She did not want to find out. Something was going to be demanded of her that she did not want to give. You know who I am. You and I have always been. And as she remembered those words something in her lurched, not away from but towards the thing that demanded. You and I. Belonging. Love me, love me, love me. To belong, to be loved, to be one.

NO! With a jerky movement she swept up the cards and the pack and slapped them together, leaving the glass as it was, alone in the middle of the table. She ran into the kitchen, reached for the dustbin, jerked up the lid, and made to throw the cards in. Then she stopped, slowly replaced the lid, and put the cards on the table. It was foolish. They were only cards, and it was not their fault. She left them and feeling suddenly cold and weary went back towards the bedroom.

The glass was only a glass, but she could not bring herself to touch it, and it was still there the next morning. She picked it up as cautiously as if it might bite and put it away in the cupboard. She did not want Gerry to know what she had been doing.

She knew she must decide soon. That morning she telephoned her doctor's surgery and made an appointment for the following afternoon.

CHAPTER SIX

Her appointment was for half past two, and it was a quarter to four when her name was called, so that she entered the doctor's room with a sense of defeat and futility.

The doctor was brisk and had a completely misleading motherly face and figure.

'Well now, what can I do for you?' she said. Agatha sat down on the chair beside the desk, and at once felt gauche, shy, stupid and a needless burden to everyone. It was simple in-built role-reaction, and she couldn't help it. She clasped her hands over her handbag in her lap, perched on the edge of the seat with her knees and feet together, and spoke in a kind of hoarse, pathetic whisper. The sight of her tattered and bulging file in front of the doctor did nothing to improve her morale. Could she really have had all that treatment in the course of a remarkably healthy life?

'You're not going to find it easy to believe

this,' she said with an attempt at being herself. The doctor smiled professionally. There was nothing of humour or even of human contact in that smile.

'We'll see,' she said. 'What's been the trouble?'

The carefully prepared speech, the logical, chronological list of symptoms she had worked up and ready in her mind abandoned her to her fate.

'I'm shrinking,' she said. She watched the doctor not reacting and cursed herself. You blown it, baby, she thought. De doc won' lissen to ya now.

'What makes you think so?' the doctor said calmly.

'My clothes don't fit any more. My trousers are all too long. I can't see my reflection in the bathroom mirror. I can't reach things off shelves. I thought at first I was just losing weight but I'm shorter as well as thinner. I'm just smaller all over.'

'Anything else?' the doctor said. She was looking into Agatha's eyes attentively but there was no contact. Christ, isn't that enough, Agatha thought, but she said,

'My hair's changed colour. It used to be dark brown.'

The doctor smiled. 'Do you know, I thought there was something different about you but I couldn't think what it was. Well, it suits you like that.'

'You don't understand. I didn't change it. I didn't dye it or bleach it. It just went blonde of its own accord. And now my eyes are changing too. I can't see so well—I have to peer. And there are dark flecks in them that are getting bigger.'

'Let's have a look,' the doctor said, getting up. Agatha was relieved that she was going to do something; every sentence she spoke pushed her further along the plank. She tilted her head back while the doctor peered into both eyes with that little silver job with the light on the end.

'Hm,' she said. 'Some kind of dark pigmentation. And you say your hair went blonde of its own accord?' She picked up a piece of it, examined, it, peered at the roots. 'It doesn't look bleached,' she murmured.

'I *told* you—'

'Yes, of course you did. And you say you've lost weight? Do you know how much?'

'A couple of stone, I should think. I don't know exactly, but I used to weigh going on ten stone.'

'Would you like to hop up on the scales now? Just slip off your shoes.'

It was eight stone two.

'I've never been eight stone two. I've never been less than nine stone in my life.'

The doctor seemed inclined to pay more attention to the weight loss than anything else. The way she skipped over Agatha's insistence that she was shrinking showed she didn't believe her. She asked a few questions about her diet, and she said,

'Any other symptoms?'

'I sleep badly. And my temper's a bit uncertain. I feel edgy and irritable, where I was always very calm and placid.'

'Are you worrying about anything in particular?'

'No,' Agatha said, defeated. She could not mention the dream, not to this doctor.

'Well, there doesn't seem to be too much wrong with you at first glance,' the doctor said after a moment. 'It's possible that the weight loss and the pigmental changes are caused by a hormonal imbalance. Are you on the Pill?'

'Yes.'

'Well, I want you to come off it for the moment, and I'll make an appointment for you to go down to the hospital and have some tests—blood and urine, that sort of thing—and we'll see if anything shows up. And then when I've got the results I'd like you to come in again. Meanwhile, I want you to weigh yourself regularly, every morning at the same time if possible, before you eat or drink anything. Can you do that?'

'Yes.'

'And make a note of it and bring the record in when you come to see me again. And I'll prescribe you a very mild tranquillizer that will just relax you. You'll find it helps you to sleep as well, although it isn't a sleeping pill.' She scribbled busily, and Agatha watched without comment. 'And we'd better arrange some sort of alternative form of birth control—'

'There's no need. I haven't got anyone at the moment. And anyway, that's another thing that's shrunk—my sexual appetite.'

The doctor looked up at that point with the first sign of interest. 'That does sound like a hormonal imbalance. These things happen after a long time on the Pill. I do like my patients to come off it for a while, but for some of them the anxiety it causes them is worse than staying on it.' She handed over the prescription. 'Have this made up. Your hospital appointment will come through the post in a day or two, and if you'll ring up for an appointment with me after you've been to the hospital—'

'Yes,' said Agatha. 'Thank you.'

Outside in the street she stretched and breathed the fresh air of normality and wondered why all laws of reason seemed suspended inside that building. She looked at the prescription in her hand. Valium. Like what the Romans dug in front of Hadrian's Wall. She screwed it up and dropped it into the next litter bin she passed.

She did not go straight home. She felt restless and uneasy, and she kept walking, along the high street, past the slumbrous mid-week shoppers, past the bus stops and

Woolworths and Family Butchers and Hygienic Bakeries and litter bins and belisha beacons and bicycles chained to safety railings and dogs waiting outside supermarkets and fruitanveg stalls against the kerbs on the corners of sidestreets. It was all normal, right, immutable. She had tramped up and down high streets like this all her life, was practically born doing it. Nothing is more unchangeably a woman's lot than doing the shopping. Nothing is more absolutely normal than the sight of a shabbily-dressed, shapeless woman walking slowly home with two battered shopping-bags stuffed with tea and marg and tins of peas and packets of biscuits. That's why women's arms were longer than men's. Patient under their loads as donkeys; planted in endless queues or at bus-stops on their bulging feet as though the grimy pavement grew them; wearers of patterned headscarves and Marks-and-Spencers dresses, purchasers of china cart-horses with real leather harness, coveters of three-piece-suites and corner-units-with-built-in-cocktail-cabinets; they were the inertia which weighted the world sufficiently to keep it spinning on its Access and prevent it from rocketing off round the galaxy like a wonky wheel.

One and yet not one of them. Nothing like this could happen to them. She put her fingers to her mouth and ran them over her lips, her livelihood. All the parameters of her life were out of kilter with the rest of the world she had known and grown up with, but at core she was a shopping-bag-carrier still. That was her trouble—traitor to herself, permanent outsider, permanent exile, like the unmated two-year-old driven out of the herd who follows it at a distance, circling the grazing area at a known but unmarked distance that could never be broached.

Would the new youngsters be like that, or was life really changing for them? Perhaps all the generations of the transition felt like her, but things would gradually improve until with the death of the last of her type the new world would be complete. One could only hope so, or what was all this fighting for? And meanwhile, her own particular problem was at hand, to be submitted to or fought. She turned on an impulse into Woolworths where there was a photo-booth, and had four mug-shots taken. She hoped it would not prove anything, but it was likely to be at least two weeks before she saw the doctor again, and she was suddenly afraid of time.

* * *

Gerry hadn't come in. They had had an argument earlier. He had tried to turn it into a quarrel, while she did not even really regard it as an argument, and in the end she had lost her temper with him and shouted and he had stormed out and he hadn't come back. She had hinted that he ought to find himself somewhere to live, that's what started it all. He seemed to regard himself as permanent lodger, and though she did not actually find him any bother, a vague sense of rectitude had driven her to try to make him face up to the situation and Life In General. She had a kind of feeling that he was using her as a mother substitute. There was something odd about his acceptance of the situation, the sleeping in her bed without any sexual commerce, and in her state of frayed nerves she was on to anything odd like a rat on a bacon rind.

Probably out getting drunk. She hoped he wouldn't wake her up when he came in because she had a hard day tomorrow—rehearsal in the morning, recording session in the afternoon, and concert in the evening, and it was quite heavy stuff too—a Prokofiev for the concert and R. Strauss for the recording. Oh my achin' lip, she thought drowsily, snuggling a little under the covers. It was nice after so long to have the bed to herself again; it was also nice to feel she was going to sleep. She was in that utterly delicious state on the brink of sleep when one is just awake enough to know how blissfully warm and comfortable one is. And then—zzzzzzz.

She woke some unknown time later to the awareness that her hair was standing on end and that every goose-pimple on her body was on tiptoe. She was lying on her back, and her nipples were standing up like guardsmen, and it was only that observation which brought it home to her fumbling mind that the covers were off her. Not slipped off sideways, but drawn down to the end of the bed, exposing her whole body to the cool night air.

And then a shriek died in her throat, her heart thudded sickeningly in her belly, as she saw Him standing there beside the bed. Unutterable terror invaded her, draining all ability to move or protest out of her, for she was wide awake, unquestionably awake, and this was no dream. *This was reality*. He smiled down at her, the faint light from the window touching his teeth as they showed between his parted lips. His compact, broad-shouldered body was a blend of light and shadow, and the shadows seemed to merge into the darkness of the room so that as he moved he seemed made of some flowing substance that ebbed and solidified, distinct but unsubstantial.

She watched his hands—broad, square hands, short-fingered but not clumsy—approach her breasts, and she shuddered as they touched her, cold and silky, their touch firm and knowing. He kneaded her breasts for a moment, and she saw his lips part to draw a stronger breath, though there was no sound of his breathing in the room, no sound at all. His hands passed down over her ribs, sliding in at her waist, and on caressively over her belly and down over her thighs, the fingers trailing along the soft inner edge. Then up again, sliding smoothly to her groin and turning inwards.

She saw now that he was breathing hard; she saw the curl of his nostrils, his lips parted over his teeth, the movement of his chest; he was excited. And she—she, though unable to move, though rigid with fear, was beginning also to warm. Inside she wanted to fight, but the fighting was a long way down, deep inside her, and retreating. His hands, gently easing her legs apart, were arousing her; something, something, whatever it was, was draining her will to resist.

Her limbs felt as heavy as if she were struggling through water, but under his hands they moved easily, spread apart, wide apart, and torpidly she watched as he climbed on to the bed and knelt between her knees. The sensation of his hands on her skin was absolutely real, and yet the bed did not dip under him, nor the sheet crease where he knelt; as if he was palpable and yet weightless.

Her head might have been nailed to the pillow, her jaws glued and wired, for all the protest she could make, and yet she managed somehow to groan a negative or at least to communicate one to him. He looked into her face, smiling. His eyes were large, yet netted round with tiny fine lines, as if he were either older than he looked, or had suffered terrible pain or sorrow. His lips moved, and though there was no sound, she heard him saying,

'Oh yes, you must let me.'

His fingers parted the lips of her vulva, and a wild sexual excitement shot through her, turning her insides to water. The voice of negation sank deeper, grew smaller, the centre of resistance shrinking in on itself while the desire of her body expanded and filled her with longing, longing for him, longing to be filled with, possessed by him. She wanted him in her, she ached for him; though the terror and horror, muted and driven down, knew it was danger. He guided his penis to her and she struggled frantically towards and away from him, though her leaden body never moved; and with a piercing sense of sensual bliss that was at the same time horrified despair, she felt him slide deliciously, hard and fully in.

Now he looked at her, leaning over her with his weight on his arms, hanging his face above her as he moved. Silently he said her name.

'Agatha, Agatha. You're lovely. I love you, Agatha. You must love me, love me, love me.'

I do, said one part of her mind, while the tiny core of herself, pinned and dying like a butterfly, screamed no no no I won't! Leave me alone! And all the while the sensual, physical delight was spreading like lapping flames through her body, making every nerve-ending quiver, driving her from the exquisite point of sensation which was his penis filling her towards an unbearable climax. She saw his face grow taut, saw his teeth grit and his eyelids flutter down as he arched above her, his head drawn back in the ecstasy of sustained pleasure. There was sound now—not from him, who seemed to exist in an uncanny bubble of silence, but from her, a laboured gasping as she dragged breath in between her rigid jaws.

Then like a rising flood the orgasm overwhelmed her, exploding like an electrical storm through every nerve, so piercing and so violent that it jerked her body up off the mattress, though the strange inertia of her limbs still prevented her from moving with it, and the conflict seemed to turn her inside out, wrenching her fibres apart, tearing her flesh from bone. At the same moment he said, cried out soundlessly,

'Oh yes! Now, Agatha, now!' and he expanded inside her until she thought he must split her open like a rotten log, and the first sound came from him, a shriek that grew and grew like a banshee wail to an ear-splitting climax as he convulsed inside her, flooding her with his own orgasm, and her soul cried out in despair. It was accomplished; and the flowing shadows and light that made up his body seemed to grow more fluid still, and in that long, frozen moment of climax he dissolved and dissipated into the darkness and she was left, flattened, exhausted, bathed in sweat, sprawled on her back on the bed, alone and helpless.

'Oh God,' she whimpered. 'Oh God.' She

could feel the wetness between her legs, but when she tried to lift her hand even that effort was beyond her. Her eyes rolled up in their sockets and she lost consciousness.

* * *

When she woke, it was daylight. She was lying in the same position, on her back, asprawl, the covers off her, and for the moment she felt so heavy and dazed she could not think what had happened. She struggled to sit up and look at the clock. It was ten to ten. Oh God, she was going to be late for rehearsal. Her head buzzed, her mouth was dry, and she felt leaden and sick, as if she had influenza. She swung her legs over the side of the bed and slumped there, dizzy, and then the memory came back to her, landing with a thump in her brain and spreading cold fear through her mind.

At first she thought it must have been a dream, all a dream; but then her own sensations told her differently—there was no mistaking that feeling of having been occupied. And then—she inspected herself. There was a light crusting on the inner surfaces of her thighs which had dried white; and inside her—She shuddered. The smell, too, of semen, was unmistakable. That part, at any rate, was real. But if he had not been flesh and bone, not substantial, how could he have filled her with real substantial semen? And if that was real, how could it have come from a thing made of shadows?

Had someone broken in? Had she been had by a real human being, her sleep-waking state making it into a dream for her? But the windows were closed and fastened on the inside, front and back doors were locked. And he had not come or gone—he had appeared and disappeared.

She began to weep, the tears running hot and bitter down her face. She felt so weak, so helpless, used and sore and heavy, weary to the bone, frightened, bewildered, alienated from herself. What was He, what was *it*, what did He want? Yet he had not abused her, nor hurt her, he had spoken kindly to her; it was her helplessness that had bruised her soul, made her feel used and soiled, and that terrible moment of struggle when the climax had racked her body as if it would snap her in pieces. She had read of how men with radiation sickness sometimes suffered nerve-storms so severe that they broke their own bones with the ferocity of their chaotic convulsions. That was how it had felt to her.

Most of all, she felt lost, as if her *self* was being parted from her, as if it was hanging over a precipice and its hands were slipping. Her *self* was being driven out. She didn't want to die; she was so afraid that she would die. Her tears fell, dripping off her fingers and spattering on her knees, warm as blood. God help me. I don't know what's happening to me.

At last habit took over. Her tears spent themselves, and she dragged herself to her feet and went to the bathroom and ran a bath and climbed in and washed the sweat and semen from her body, washed her hair (not her hair) and scrubbed her teeth, and then, clean and dry and smelling more like herself, she pulled on a pair of jeans and a tee-shirt and a pair of sandals, grabbed her trumpet case, and went out to the car. She felt as though she had not slept at all, and it was twenty past ten, and even if she drove as fast as she could, she was still going to be forty minutes late, and there would be trouble. She could guess what Malcolm would say, and if he was horrible to her she would probably cry, and that would only exasperate him and shame her. All of a sudden, she felt trapped and desperate, like a rabbit baring its teeth at a fox.

And as she roared along the embankment she wondered what had happened to Gerry.

* * *

The concert finished at ten to ten, and they got out by ten. She and one or two others went to the current local pub for a drink, and by that time she was feeling much better. The tiredness of a day's work had driven out the unnatural tiredness that had gripped her that morning, and the event of the previous night had receded so far as to seem preposterously dreamlike and remote. She was even beginning to doubt whether she really had seen and smelled semen at all. Surely it was more likely to have been the product of an overwrought imagination? And the whole possession-episode had been a dream, hallucination, imagination, what you will. It did not match up with any pattern of reality in her brain and therefore her brain, with a day of normality under its belt, rejected it.

They crowded into the bar, filling it with their large personalities and their instrument cases. It was a tiny pub, and had nothing in particular to distinguish it from any other filling station around those parts, but for the moment none of them would dream of drinking anywhere else. The local pub changed from time to time. Everyone would crowd into the Rose and Crown week after week for a year or so, and then suddenly, without any warning or reason, by some strange process of unspoken consent, the Rose and Crown would be deserted and everyone would pile into the White Hart. Their presence was not always welcomed at first. Often the 'regulars' resented them, and the fact that nine out of every ten of them was immovably wedded to a bulky instrument case which got in everyone's way and tripped up the potman made them unpopular; but soon enough the pub would settle down to its one or two-year reign, until some changing tide of musicians' fancy left it beached and abandoned and they all crammed themselves into the snug at the King's Head or the saloon bar at the Prince of Wales.

They were still negotiating the purchase of the first round when someone bellowed over the heads to Agatha, who was pressed up against the bar relaying orders,

'Hey, Aggie, your gigolo's here! Says he wants a pint.'

She managed to turn her head and saw young Gerry, towering above most of the others in the bar, standing near the door, looking at her with the hesitant smile of a dog with feathers round its mouth. She smiled back reassuringly, and saw his shoulders relax. Be damned to his role play. If he wanted a mother, let him go back to the one nature had provided him with; she was not going to ask him where he'd been all night. By the time the round had been bought and distributed and she had worked her way eel-like to the corner where he was standing he had made the adjustment, and greeted her with a cheerful,

'Hello, had a good day?'

'Busy. Were you at the concert?'

'No, I went down to Maidenhead to see my Grandma. Spent the day there. You've never seen so many antique shops in one place. You'd think they were breeding. I don't know how any of them makes a living, but Grandma seems to do all right.'

'Has she got an antique shop, then?'

'Yes; well, sort of. I mean she does have some antiques, but mostly it's bric-à-brac and curios and other junk like that. I had a nice time sorting through some boxes of postcards while she was serving some military type. You know, real old seaside picture-postcards. And some marvellous old photographs, all brown and curly. I kind of took a fancy to one. Dunno why really. I brought it back for you. Here—prezzy.'

He offered it with a half-apologetic smile that told her it was, or had been intended as, a peace offering. She took it in the spirit in which it was offered. Mounted on thick card, it had survived its ages well, a sepia-tint photograph of a man in a tight suit and a very high collar, Edwardian, or perhaps Victorian, she wasn't all that good on costume. A youngish man—

She stared, and her hand seemed to freeze into a claw, like those tiny grabcranes at the fairground that you worked with a sixpence, that always missed the prizes you wanted and seized immovably on to a chewing-gum-ball and a pink plastic bracelet.

She stared and the photograph stared back. A young man with strangely old eyes standing very stiffly in a photographer's favourite pose, one foot forward, one hand on the back of an over-stuffed chair.

It was Him.

CHAPTER SEVEN

'But that makes it better for you, doesn't it?' Gerry said.

'Better? What do you mean better?' Agatha stared in amazement.

'I mean that it proves it isn't all just your imagination. What it means is that this is a real ghost. We ought to tell someone about it.'

'Don't you dare tell anyone!'

'Calm down, I meant the Society for Psychical Research or whatever they're called. They'd be really excited, I bet you.'

'It proves nothing,' Agatha said wearily. Gerry grew agitated.

'But look, it's such a coincidence—and that I should pick out that picture of all pictures—and he must have been a real person and he must now be dead, so that makes him a ghost, and—'

'But you only have my word for it that the ghost looks like him,' Agatha said patiently, as to an idiot. 'And as to coincidences, they're coming in rather too large a size. Isn't it much more likely that I only imagine that is a photograph of the man I imagine I see? Much more likely than that blind chance has thrust a photograph of him into a stranger's hand to be brought by some miracle to my notice.'

Gerry looked hurt. 'Then you think—'

'I'm telling you what others would think, and what's likely. I've never seen that photo before, but I've seen that face before. It's the face that comes to my bedside night after night.'

He observed how white and tired she looked. Her face looked older, she was changed even to him. He tried to sound reassuring. 'Anyway, now I'm back he won't be bothering you again. He didn't come before when I slept in with you, did he?'

She looked at him, and he hurried on, 'All right, but it'll prove something one way or the other. I mean if he comes you can wake me and we'll see if I can see him. And if he doesn't—'

'Yes, if he doesn't?'

'Well, you know, it could be your imagination, couldn't it?' he said awkwardly. She looked at him sadly.

'Do you think I hadn't thought of that?'

All the same, she was a little comforted. She thought that the ghost would not come while Gerry was there; but she was afraid that he would come and Gerry would not be able to see him. On the whole she would prefer haunting to mental illness, seeing that the ghost was basically benign. She made them both cocoa when they got in, and the soothing associations combined with the drink she had had made her pleasantly sleepy. She made a hot-water-bottle for extra comfort and they got into bed.

Gerry was asleep quickly, with the ease of young animals, but as soon as the light was out she found herself wide awake again and restless, her mind running over and over the evidence and the possibilities. The man in the photograph—who was he? There was no name on the back, except the name of the photographer, J. Miles of Paradise Road, Richmond; presumably the man had lived in Richmond. One did not go far from home for a photograph, did one? But there was little to be gained from that information. Even if the business of J. Miles was still in operation, they would not have a record of a photograph taken so long ago.

How long ago? she wondered. If only she were better on costume and period furniture. But say that it was turn-of-the-century, to be vague and conservative in both directions; the man looked about thirty, which would mean he would have been dead probably about forty years. Was that enough for a ghost? She had an idea they had to be dead a long time to begin haunting. But that was absurd—who could make a ghost obey rules? And in any case, *why her*? There had to be some kind of reason even to unreason.

She had not told Gerry everything. She could not tell anyone that. He would not come again now that Gerry was here. Or at least, she would not imagine him to come again.

She must have fallen asleep, because she came awake with a violent jerk, so violent that the lurch of her heart frightened her, as if it might damage itself. Then slowly, like a radio tuning in, she became aware of cold hands on her shoulders, cold lips on her face kissing her gently, and the voice that had no sound very close to her saying,

'Agatha, at last, at last.'

No, go away, she cried inwardly.

'Let me, darling, let me in. Oh *yes*!'

He was lying on top of her, his body against hers all the way down; he was barely taller than her. There was a sensation of pressure, but no weight. Where their flesh touched, it was cold and then quickly warm, as if the substance he was made of took warmth from her. The hands, the lips were palpable, but he was made only of shadows and light. She managed to lift her head a fraction, and she could see her own body through it, except where the darkest shadows were. She could not lift her hands, nor move, nor struggle, except inside herself, in her soul.

'Who are you?' she cried, and she heard her own voice, no more than a hoarse whisper, but at least audible. She had broken from him that much. 'What do you want with me? Leave me alone.'

'I won't hurt you, Agatha,' he said. It did not sound like an answer, but like an automatic reaction. 'Oh let me, darling; love me. You must love me. We have so little time.'

'Let me *alone*! What do you want of me? Why me? Who are you? Oh go away, *please*!' She began to grow desperate as she felt herself weakening, felt her strength, like her body's warmth, being drained into his shadowy substance. Tears filled her eyes and rolled out helplessly and down her rigid face. 'Please don't,' she heard herself whisper, pitifully, hopelessly. The hands were parting her thighs, the body nudging down between her legs. The man lifted his head, tilting his face back to look down at her, and he smiled.

'It's all right,' he said. 'Don't cry.' At least, she knew he had said it, though his lips did not move, and there was no sound in the air beyond her own uneven breathing of fear and distress. His hands were feeling for her, parting the way, guiding his erect penis to her. She struggled madly, and his smile was the smile of the kindly predator, the smile of every man who had ever said to an apprehensive girl, don't worry, you'll enjoy it.

'Oh no, oh no, please no!' As she felt him begin to penetrate her, her fear grew more frantic, and she struggled more violently, growing almost demented as she felt the smooth possession being accomplished, felt her traitor body begin to quiver with involuntary, horrible pleasure. She struggled so wildly that she managed to move a hand, though it did no more than twitch; her fingers, flexing with the last residue of that blanketed effort, touched the warm sleeping bulk of Gerry.

Gerry! Of course, Gerry! He would save her!

Why didn't he wake? Oh God, oh God, wake!

'Gerry! Help me! Help me!'

Her voice no more than a whisper, a faint murmur, while her body moved up to meet each inward stroke of her destruction. I don't want, but I want. The growing physical pleasure, the sensual excitement running along her nerves was sapping her will. I must not want, I do want. Gerry wake, why don't you wake? How can you sleep while *this* is going on? He was growing harder, moving faster, moving in towards the climax, and she was melting, her resistance dispersing, moving to meet him, going with him.

No! With a heart-tearing effort she turned her head on the pillow, dragging it round as if she were pulling the flesh off her own bones, and her mouth moving slowly and numbly as if underwater managed only a distorted underwater cry, but she called him, Gerry! Wake! And saw him, lying on his back, asleep, peacefully, a slight frown of concentration on his face as if sleep were a purposeful business. And her heart despaired in her, knowing she was lost.

The cold lips touched her cheek, the hands

turned her face back, and the lips were on hers, the tongue pushing into her mouth with that strange, remote, silent, cold passion; she was near the climax, her body washed in ecstasy that was both intense and languorous, he was swollen and hard inside her, every movement touching new veins of exquisite pleasure, and she knew that what he wanted what he was asking love me love me love me was possible was imminent and that was the treachery of herself to herself not the surrendering but the wanting to. Oh no please no she moaned but no longer aloud and not to him and not with any hope. Her body lifted filled flowered outwards with agonized bliss and the triumph of accomplishment and her hands lifted from her sides where they had been helpless but only to fold around him around his intangible shadowy realer-than-reality and the cry that came from her tortured lungs was a long o of perfect submission and love.

Shadows flowed and the presence inside her subsided became insubstantial dispersed dislimned and she cried out with the sense of loss. Her body lay abandoned, spent, as limp and empty as an empty glove, and she was nothing, she was lost, no more herself. So unutterable was her sense of loss that she could not cry or move; all that was alive of her was one coldly burning point at the quick of her where *He* had been, and the life in her was his not hers; He was; she was not.

What has happened to me? But the question died in her mind even as she asked it, for she was no more. Bitter, black despair washed through her, and she fell through the void like a falling star, falling, falling, falling until the emptiness closed over her and she slept the sleep of the exhausted.

* * *

Polly picked her up at Henry Wood Hall at lunchtime and they went to the King's Arms in Roupell Street for a pint and a sandwich.

'You look wrecked,' Polly said bluntly. 'Have you been making a night of it?'

Agatha tensed. 'Don't start,' she said.

'Bad night?' Agatha nodded. 'Nightmares again?'

Agatha hesitated. She could not tell Gerry; dared she tell Polly? She wanted, badly, to talk about it, but—

'I dreamt about that man again. That he came in and screwed me.'

'Screwed you? How d'you mean? Raped you?'

Agatha shrugged, glad Polly had not made more fuss. 'I don't know. In a way, yes—but it wasn't violent. Just that I couldn't move or cry out.'

'I know dreams like that. I dream I'm chasing someone and my legs won't move.'

Agatha laughed explosively. 'Typical! Anyone else would have dreamt they were being chased, but not Polly.'

'Well it sounds rather nice, dreaming of sex. I wish I could. I can't even get it in reality.'

'Poor Pol. Brian playing you up?'

She nodded glumly. 'He said he couldn't see me because he had to go and see the children. It was Tara's birthday—'

'Tara?'

'True, I'm afraid.'

'Oh Pol, how can you love a man who calls his daughter Tara?'

Polly grinned suddenly, her self peeping out from under the love-affair that tended to blot her out. 'His son's called Jason.'

'Lordy!'

'Anyway, he said he had to go and see them, and I was a bit cross that he hadn't remembered before because it put *my* evening out, but I thought well he's got to go and see the brat, fair enough, so I didn't make a fuss.'

'You know that's where you go wrong, don't you? I mean, just look at your previous experiences, and mine come to that. If you behave reasonably, like a proper human being, and treat them as equals, they take the most shameful advantages. The women they treat well are the real ratbags who behave as badly as possible and make terrible scenes over nothing.'

'True. But what can we do? I couldn't be unreasonable if I tried. And it wouldn't be me, anyway, would it?'

'Nor me. I can't get away from this ridiculous notion that there should be honesty in a relationship, and that if he doesn't like me as I am he won't do. So I won't dissemble, not on major issues anyway. Pol, you know this bloke isn't good enough for you.'

'He happens to be the one I want,' she said tautly, and Agatha was warned. 'You're right though. Your Phil runs off with a woman who'll stand on his neck and tell him what to do, and that George of yours was devoted to that terrible wife who went through his pockets and called the police if he was five minutes late in rush-hour.'

'We've got it wrong, old girl. But anyway, finish telling me about Brian.'

'Oh yes—well, he said he'd come round to my place on the way home, and I was quite pleased with that, because I really felt like a screw, so I did a bit of work and then had a bath and washed my hair and all that sort of thing, and then he didn't come and he didn't come and finally, get this, at twenty to one, he telephoned from Janice's flat—'

'Not really!'

'He didn't say that's where he was, but I know he was because I could hear the dog barking in the background, and she's got one of those beastly little Yorkshire terriers. And he said he was sorry he couldn't make it but something had cropped up. So I said wasn't it a bit rude to refer to Janice as something, and he went very quiet for a minute, and then he said he was sorry but she'd phoned up at his wife's house and she was very upset and crying and everything and demanded he went round to see her. Apparently someone had told her about me—'

'Told her about you? You mean *he* hadn't told her?'

Polly stared bitterly into her pint. 'No, he hadn't told her,' she said heavily. 'So much for the honest man. I spoke to him again this morning. I couldn't say too much last night because I was too upset. He said he couldn't tell her about me because it would upset her too much. So I said was he in love with her, and he said not really but that she was terribly fond of him and sort of depended on him. So I told him that in that case it was all the more important that he let her know as soon as possible that he didn't return her feelings, but he just sort of shuffled and said he *couldn't*. He kept saying he didn't want to hurt anybody, so I just yelled "Don't, then."'

'Oh Polly,' Agatha said. She had heard it all, all before. Polly looked up with a wry smile.

'Oh you haven't heard the worst yet. I discovered afterwards from Costos—you know he's Brian's friend— that he didn't tell Janice even last night. He spent the night convincing her that it was all lies about him and me.'

'But—he was telephoning you from her flat—'

'He didn't tell her that. He told her that he'd promised to go and see his mother and had to phone to explain why he hadn't come. I *thought* he sounded odd on the phone—the way he was talking—but I assumed it was because he felt guilty. His *mother*—' she finished disgustedly.

'Polly, after this surely—'

'I don't want to give him up,' she said abruptly, and that was that. She was lost in thought for a moment, and then roused herself to say, 'But never mind about my dreary problems. What about yours? When do you see the doctor again?'

'Next week. I don't suppose it will get us anywhere, though. I have no faith in the tests showing anything up, and the doctor was quite clearly of the opinion that I was imagining everything.'

'Did you tell her about the dreams?'

'No. They weren't serious then, and in any case, I didn't want her thinking I was a head case. It was hard enough telling her I was shrinking—'

'But Ag, you are,' Polly said quietly. They looked at each other cautiously. 'Don't you notice I'm looking down at you now, and you used to be a bit taller than me if anything.'

'*I* notice,' Agatha said.

'And your eyes—'

'They aren't shrinking.'

'Don't joke. I know you're scared shitless inside. They used to be blue. Then they were blue with brown flecks. Now they're brown with blue flecks.'

'I know,' Agatha said with dark humour. 'I've been looking. Oh God, Polly, what can be happening to me? I've never heard of anything like this before. And now these dreams—I can't sleep, and when I wake up in the morning I feel absolutely fucked.' It was not quite a joke.

'Tired?'

'Not just tired. Sort of drained. Less as though I'd missed a night's sleep than as if I'd been working really hard—digging the garden or something. I'm worn out, Pol, and I'm terrified my work's going to suffer. Malc keeps on looking sideways at me; I know he's just waiting for me to slip up.'

'Bastard!'

'No, not really. I don't mean he wants me to. In a way it's the opposite—he's terrified that I will. He doesn't want there to be any excuse to sack me, and he knows—Christ, we all know—that the board would be very happy to see me put down. I'm the only female trumpet player in a first class orchestra at the moment, and they don't like it. They didn't want women in the orchestra at all, and they'd be only too glad to see their theories proved right, that women aren't as good, aren't reliable, allow their emotions to interfere with their work—you know all the old cliches.'

'Don't I just,' Polly said fervently.

'And the horrible thing is, maybe they're right. Look at me—in bits because of a nightmare. My work hasn't suffered yet, because I won't let it. But how long can I live on my will? I *will* go on playing, but it's only my will that is keeping me together, and that's being sapped. It's wearing me out, the fight. I keep wanting to give in, and one day I know I will.'

'Give in to who? Gerry?' Polly was puzzled. Agatha laughed, and Polly heard the edge of hysteria there.

'Gerry! Christ, no! The ghost, Pol, or whatever he is. I feel myself wanting to give in to him, to lie down and stop fighting. It's like slipping down a slippery slope, a little more each day, and the further you slip the less likely you are to be able to get back up. But I *will not* give in.' Her fists clenched, and Polly saw how they trembled, saw how frighteningly grim her face became as she clenched her teeth, asserting her will against the fear and the disintegration. 'I am myself, and I will not give in.'

Polly wanted to touch her, in comfort, but she refrained, seeing how close to the edge her friend was, fearing that to touch her might break her hold on herself and she said sadly, seeing for a moment behind some barriers she had erected for herself, ‘I think that’s what they all want; to break us. They don’t want us to be ourselves, to have identity outside of them. It frightens them. That’s why they don’t like us, Ag, and they don’t, do they? You and I and all our friends like us—we scare them because we don’t belong to them. And the Janices of this world—they do what’s expected of them, they play the role and get the applause.’

Agatha stared at her. ‘I never thought you would see it, Pol.’

‘But the trouble is, I keep wanting to get into the play. I keep doing auditions, don’t I? I want to have a Janice-part, and if that means giving up myself and becoming—’

‘You can’t become.’

‘Oh yes I could.’ Polly was grave with the new awareness. ‘I could easily. Is it wrong to want to?’

‘I don’t know what’s right and wrong. If you think it’s wrong, then it’s wrong, that’s all.’

‘I don’t know if I do or not. I keep changing my mind about that, according to circumstances. When I have him, I want to be me, and when I don’t, I want to give in so that I can get him back. And giving in would be shameful, wouldn’t it?’

‘For me, not shameful, but the end. In the end, when everything’s been taken away from you, and you’re standing in a pile of rubble faced with the task of starting all over again to put one stone on top of another, all you have left is your pride. I've had to rebuild three times already, and the foundations of this house are pretty rocky. If I lose my sense of myself now, I've had it.'

Polly could say nothing. She was afraid, because she heard the grim, grey truth in Agatha's voice. That was no melodrama, it was a statement of fact from a level-headed woman standing on the brink of the chasm; the freckled eyes were the eyes of one who has seen the end come into sight.

'Agatha, who is he, this man you dream about?' Agatha did not correct the word 'dream'. In any case, she had no vocabulary to cover the kind of reality He was.

'I don't know. I wish I did—then I might know what he wants, and how I can resist.'

'Do you think he might be something to do with your mother? I mean, there must be some reason for it, and he doesn't come out of your life. How much do you know about your mother?'

'Virtually nothing. But he can't have been her lover if that's what you're thinking—the age is wrong.'

'What do you mean, the age is wrong?' Polly asked. Agatha told her about the photograph, and she grew excited.

'But if he really existed, and you never knew him, it proves it's a real haunting, not just your imagination,' she said, much as Gerry had.

Agatha let it go. 'If the age is wrong for him to have been her lover, he could have been some other connection with her. He could have been her father, couldn't he?'

'Why would he want to screw me, if he's my grandfather?' Agatha said.

'Well how should I know?' Polly said explosively. 'But there must be some reason why he picks on you. Is there some way you could find out about your mother? Have you any relatives you could ask? You might pick up a clue.'

'I've no relatives that I know of. You know I was taken out from the rubble, and my mother was dead. I never heard that she had anyone in the world. If she'd had any relatives I imagine they would have taken me in, rather than leave me in an orphanage.'

'But someone must have known her. Someone must have identified the body, a friend or a neighbour. Maybe they'd know, if they're still alive. They might give you some hint.'

'And in any case,' Agatha finished the thought for her, 'just the feeling that I was doing something would be a kind of therapy, wouldn't it?'

Polly shrugged. 'Why not?'

'But do you realize how much work would be involved in trying to trace someone like that? And you know how I'm fixed for spare time.'

'Get Gerry to do all the leg-work,' Polly said easily. 'He'd do anything for you. And it would get him out from under your feet, and use up some of the energy you say you aren't using up for him. By the way, have you thought that it might be Gerry who screwed you in the night?'

'Yes, the thought occurred to me—but it wasn't. I told you I could see him sleeping, quite clearly. And in any case, he wouldn't, and if he did he'd remember it the next day. No, that horse won't run, Pol.'

'I thought you were going to say that cock won't fight.'

'That is another form of the expression, I believe,' Agatha said gravely. 'But just in case he wakes up when I'm being visited, I'm not going to have him in with me any more.'

'I should have thought you'd be glad to have him wake up.'

'Then you thought wrong,' she said sharply. 'I don't want him to witness *that*. I don't want *anyone—*'

'All right, don't bite. Want another?'

'Better not, I'm on again at two. Don't want to give the anti-Agatha brigade ammunition.'

Polly raised an eyebrow. 'When I want a drink, I have a drink. No one tells me what to do.'

They had another drink.

CHAPTER EIGHT

The day before her doctor's appointment a fixer she sometimes did work for phoned her up and asked her to do two out-of-town dates, one in Birmingham and one in Manchester, on the two subsequent days. The programme was Berlioz' Roman Carnival and Bruch's violin concerto, and since the fixer wanted her to play first cornet in the one and first b-flat in the other, it would be a pretty lucrative date: as well as the concert fee she'd get two principal's fees.

'Too good to turn down,' she told Gerry. 'Especially the way things are at the moment.' Everyone was short of engagements for August.

'I still think you ought to go to the doctor,' Gerry said.

'Don't mother me,' she said, managing to sound pleasant. 'I can go to the doctor any time.'

'All right.' He recognized the tension in her voice. 'While you're away, I'll see what I can find out. I'll go down to Somerset House. Unless,' wistfully, 'you want me to come to Birmingham with you?'

Agatha grinned. 'You are kidding! Can you imagine what would be said if I turned up with you in the car? My reputation is already made.'

*   *   *

Hotel rooms, the same the world over, amorphous, unreal, little bubbles existing outside reality. Tasteless wallpaper, furniture carefully treated so that the wood looked like plastic, nylon carpets with fidgety little patterns, central-heating, the walk from the lift through windowless corridors smelling of carpet dust, the muffled sounds coming from no particular direction of other people living their mysterious transitions between realities behind precisely similar doors in precisely similar rooms.

Here at least, surely, she must be safe? Rehearsal from five to six, then a bite to eat and a drink with Marcus Maylin, the young second trumpet, and Stan Wilberforce and Bill Luton, two of the trombones, then the concert from seven-thirty to just after nine, back to the hotel for several more drinks with Marcus, who was also staying there, and a couple of woodwind players who had been borrowed from the London circuit. All getting pretty well treeless; she had gently to disentangle herself from Marcus who thought she was going to take him to bed; then to her room, fumbling a little with the key, either because she was drunk or because her eyes were playing her up again.

Too drunk and sleepy to shower. Shower in the morning. Drunk enough to sleep anyway. Arrange an alarm call with the hotel switchboard. Clothes off, dropped on the chair, in between the deliciously clean and starched sheets (best thing about hotels really, all the clean linen that someone else would launder) and sleep.

But he was there, she knew it,

in the darkness as soon as she turned off the light and before she fell asleep she knew he was there.

followed her?

Sleep. Oblivion.

And waking, terrified, not knowing where she was, her mind staggering. What year is it? What has happened so far?

Who am I? There was emptiness where things ought to be, mind furniture, no name or even shape for herself, no knowledge of her own past, let alone the present, and she sat up in bed, clawing at the darkness, gasping for breath because the blankness of her mind stopped her breathing.

Who? Where am I?

Oh God, yes, Birmingham. The word Birmingham that slid into her frantic scrabbling mind released the flood of information; it poured into the black hole inside her brain and lapping up to the natural level, the water-mark. Yes, everything was there, it was all right.

Plus.

She was not alone. The hair lifted on her skull—she felt it, felt the cool air touch her scalp where the hair rose. There was no sound of breathing, but He was there in the darkness. She reached with an icy hand for the light switch

but never reached it a hand closed over hers and pulled it down a hand she knew no human being she had ever met had a hand like that short broad thick-fingered and incredibly silky-skinned

oh no she moaned and heard her voice aloud so she could speak this time? Oh no please don't please leave me alone but the covers were being drawn off her and he was already kneeling on the bed his hands holding her by the wrists so that her arms were up on the pillows drawing her body taut his head dipping his mouth finding her nipple and suckling

oh God

hard so that the tugging went right down into her womb and she felt the maddening delicious thump right in the roots of her. He left her nipple let go her hands and moved down his face rubbing lightly over her belly down to her pubis to her already hard clitoris and his cold mouth found her out. She felt the weakness flooding her, felt her resistance going. She lifted her hands from behind her on the pillow and they came up slowly as if she were drowning Helle lifting them from the water in supplication weighted down with the darkness like water and already it was too late his head was up and his fingers parting the way his hard cool smooth penis nudging its way in like an animal burrowing into its own place and she was

parting before him like water welcoming oh God the feeling of him in her was indescribable the sense of being possessed filled completed she was incomplete without him now and yet her will, frantic, struggled, in the dark water crying inaudibly as it watched the lights of the ship pass further and further away help receding into the darkness and she would *drown*!

Her arms came up her hands reached for him he was moving now more urgently pressing into her and she could hear (no sound) his little cries of pleasure of mounting ecstasy his face above her suddenly clear though it was dark she could see him

his dear face

sweet with the pain of loving

his dear face

and she heard her mind begin to form the words I love you and her hands that had gone up to his shoulders with such effort to try to push him away were grown suddenly tender and were cupping round his face because he was so lovely so vulnerable in his love for her so needy of her and she

loved him

sweet oh sweet

the delicate delicious tremulous feelings

lapping through her opening her to his tender possession of her opening to him so that he could flow into her body expanding inside her like some dark sweet force opening up her soul her self and oh the exquisite painful delight of surrendering to him—

She gasped aloud, heard him cry out as he came in her and though her traitor hands were still cupping his face which they loved still some hard core of herself said *no*! as she felt him flow into her felt his face grow unsubstantial the pressure of him upon her disperse as his shadowy reality grew thin and dissipated and as her body ached with loss she felt also coming back through the darkness the quality of *his* loss that she had denied him and she felt

shame?

guilt?

that she had been so cruel as to deny him what he wanted.

She lay sprawled, exhausted, so heavy with weariness she could not move even to cover herself though the air struck chill upon her flesh. Even here, she thought, I am not safe; not safe anywhere, ever again, because it is me that is haunted, not the house. He wants me, and he will come back for ever and ever until I give in, and I will give in, in the end. Almost tonight, I almost said I love you and I almost did. He wants me, and he will not give up, and wouldn't it be easier to yield, would there not be pleasure, safety, comfort? What would I lose? Why not give up?

She stirred, exhausted and angry, and she pressed on that anger, blew on it like a last glowing ember because she knew, just as she knew that the possession of her body was unnatural, that that anger was *her*.

I will not, because *I* say I will not. That's all.

*   *   *

The alarm call woke her, and she fumbled for the telephone, her eyes glued together with exhaustion. Yes, thank you. She put the phone down, and dragged herself out of bed into the bathroom and under the shower. The water was very hot, and stimulated her sluggish blood. She washed her face in very hot water, and then climbed out, dried herself, and went to the sink to wash her teeth. That always helped, having clean teeth. She leaned her weight on her hands on the basin and stared into the mirror. A brown-eyed, blonde-haired woman she barely recognized stared back, a little blurred because the brown-eyed woman was short-sighted.

Agatha began to scream, and though she heard herself quite impartially as if she were someone else doing it she couldn't stop.

I looked into the mirror and the reflection I saw was not my own.

She screamed and went on screaming even

after the thunder of raps on the room door, even after the noises and shouts in the corridor, even after she heard the key in the lock and a terrified room-maid came hesitantly in with several other people cautiously at her shoulder. Only when the maid touched her did she stop. She turned and saw her own appalled fright mirrored in the maid's eyes, and then, blessedly, she lost consciousness.

* * *

It did not take a great deal of effort to get them to leave her alone. She told them she had been sleep-walking and having a nightmare, and since she spoke so clearly and sanely, they were only too happy not to have the responsibility of her. The fainting she put down to lack of food. She got herself out of there as quickly as possible, hoping against hope that Marcus would not get to hear of it. She dressed, packed, and checked out, and stopped for food at a transport cafe on the way to Manchester, and only when she was on her second cup of tea after the huge and hot fried breakfast did she stop trembling and gather her depleted forces together. She had another rehearsal and concert to do tonight, and she must do them well. If she cocked it up, it would be obvious to everyone; that was the trouble with playing the trumpet, you couldn't fake, you were right out front, and everyone heard what you did, right or wrong. She would not allow herself to think of the night that would follow.

She went to the loo in the cafe before continuing her journey and looked at herself cautiously in the chipped and spotty mirror. It was all right, really. That was her face, though it seemed strange and a little unlike her own. She recognized it. She had been overwrought that morning. It would be all right. She would not stay another night in a hotel, she would drive home after the concert. Sooner that than—

* * *

When she got home, there was a letter waiting for her from the doctor. One of the tests needed to be done again and would she present herself at the hospital on Friday at nine o'clock and make an appointment for the following week with the doctor. She would. Gerry said,

'I've done a bit of sleuthing for you, though I didn't get very far. I say, you look a bit rough. Working too hard?'

'Much too hard. Let's have a drink and you can tell me about it.'

'I don't want anything. I'll get you one though. Whisky?'

She took off her shoes and got into the big armchair, pulling her feet under her, and let him bring her a scotch. She was grateful for his presence, glad he still wanted to minister to her, pleased to be comforted by him. She felt scooped out and sore inside, as if someone had been digging out her soul with a spoon, like eating a melon.

'I got a squint at the death certificate, and the body was identified by a Miss Eleanor Thoday, status friend of deceased, and the address was 27 Kensington Avenue. I went round there—it's just a couple of streets away from where your house was, did you know that? In the back end of Notting Hill, sort of between there and Ladbroke Grove.'

'I know where you mean. Did you go there as well?'

'Yes, but of course the house isn't there now. There's quite a gap, must have been three or four houses came down in the blast, and there's a new block of flats there, not a big block, just three storeys tall, and the old houses on either side.'

'And what was Kensington Avenue like?'

'Big old houses with steps up to the front door and a basement area. Three storeys, porch with pillars over the front door. You know the kind of thing. All turned into tatty flats and bedsitters now, lots of bells with paper labels stuck on them with names like Khan and Obote.'

'And no Miss Thoday.'

'No. I rang all the bells and asked everyone

that answered if they knew of a Miss Thoday.'

'Did you? That was brave of you.'

'I got quite hopeful about the old dame in the basement. She looked about a hundred and ten, but I think she was either deaf or bonkers. She didn't seem to know what I was talking about. I think I managed to get through to her in the end. She said she didn't know anything, and I think that was about the mark. But of course she may simply have forgotten.'

'So one way or another it was a dead end.'

'Yup. But I didn't give up. I thought if this Thoday dame lived in Notting Hill and got married, then her marriage certificate would be in the London registry. I knew she was a Miss in 1944, so if she married it was after that date. Which only gave me thirty-odd years to try.'

'You went back to Somerset House?'

'Yes, except that it isn't now. And I found a marriage certificate for her. She married a bloke called Albert George Walken in 1947. It didn't help much as far as she was concerned because it gave the same address for her. But I took down his address, and I can try that.'

'You really are amazing,' Agatha said with admiration. 'All that effort.'

'I enjoyed it,' he admitted. 'It was like reading other people's diaries. I started to build up a picture of this woman, and I started spinning all sorts of daydreams round her, filling in her life for her. It was nice.'

'You should have been a writer. You realize, of course, that it's highly unlikely that they will still be living at his address—if they ever did. Single men in those days tended to live with their parents or in lodgings. They'd have got a new place when they married, more likely than not.'

'Yes, I know, but there might be someone in the street that remembers them or knows where they've gone. And I can go through the registry again and see if they had any children registered—that would give an address.'

'But if they moved out of London—?'

'And I still haven't tried all the other houses in Kensington Avenue yet. Or the other houses in Heath Road. Nil desperandum, old thing.'

'The very thought of it exhausts me,' Agatha said. 'But if you like doing it—'

'I do. It's fun. Of course, if I find this Thoday dame, you'll have to interview her. She'd hardly tell me anything about your ma, me being a stranger.'

Agatha smiled wryly. 'If you find her, I'll talk to her. If you find her, it'll be a miracle, and that'll be the least I can do. I suppose you tried looking in the telephone directory?'

His face went scarlet. 'I hadn't thought of that.' He dashed out of the room and returned with the S-Z volume. 'Luckily,' he said as he thumbed for the page, 'Walken isn't a very popular name. Think if she'd married a bloke called Williams.' He found the page and ran a finger down it, and then shook his head. 'Four Walkdens, two Walkes and a hundred million Walkers, but no Walken.'

'Pity,' she said. His face cheered up instantly.

'Never mind. It doesn't prove anything. They may not have a phone. Or they may have moved out of London.'

'If they have, you'll have a lot of trouble finding them. Well, I'm going to bed now. Listen, Gerry, I don't want you to sleep with me any more. I'll make you up a bed in the spare room, where you were before.'

'Why?' he said, going red again, this time with either distress or embarrassment.

'I don't want you to, that's all.'

'But what if you have the nightmare again?'

'Then I'll have it. Nothing's going to stop it.'

'All right, if you're sure. But leave your door open, so that I can hear you if you call out. And I'll pop in during the night to see if you're all right.'

'I wish you wouldn't,' she said irritably.

'It'll make me feel better. I worry about you,' he said. He was so absurdly young, she thought, and his dignity was precious to him. She must not laugh at him, not ever.

'All right,' she said wearily. 'If it makes you happy.' She did not think he would wake once he was asleep anyway—he slept very heavily. And if he did, and came in, he would not see anything. Would he? But she was too tired to worry about it. She wanted to sleep. The fear of what was going to happen during the night was there under the surface, but her own tiredness blunted its sharpness. And in any case, what was there she could do about it?

She went to bed and slept lightly and restlessly. Gerry, to her astonishment, did wake, and came in three times during the night, just stood in the doorway looking at her for a moment. Each time she pretended to be asleep, breathing steadily so that he would know she was not restless; and the dream, the ghost, whatever it was, did not come. Perhaps Gerry's presence disturbed it, prevented it from manifesting itself. If so, it must be the fact that he was awake that did it, because it had had no trouble materializing when he was there and asleep. Towards dawn she fell into a deeper sleep, and she woke at half past seven feeling better than she had done for weeks—still tired, but not beaten or hopeless.

At breakfast Gerry said,

'How did you sleep? I came in during the night and you seemed to be quite peaceful.'

'I didn't have the nightmare,' she said. 'I got quite a bit of sleep, in patches. I feel a lot better.'

'You look a lot better,' he said. 'Maybe having me in the bed disturbed you.'

It was generous of him to say that, considering that was where he wanted to be, and she smiled at him affectionately.

'You're a good friend,' she said, managing in time not to say 'good boy' which would have sounded dreadful, although it was what she meant. He beamed with pleasure.

'You're looking much more yourself this morning,' he said.

When she went up to comb her hair she looked at herself in the mirror and remembered his words. The face that looked back at her did not seem strange. She recognized it for her own, and she laughed aloud, thinking that his words were literally true. Perhaps there was a way back through the Labyrinth? Perhaps Gerry's search could provide the Clue?

'I am much more like my old self this morning,' she said aloud, with a hint of triumph, and she went downstairs whistling cheerfully. The house seemed full of sunshine, no shadows anywhere.

CHAPTER NINE

She knew there would be nowhere to park at the hospital so she went up by tube, hoping that she could get seen early because she was on at eleven, and if she got through quickly she could go home and get the car, otherwise she would have to go on to the studios by tube. She had her hooter with her anyway. It was heavy, but her arm was accustomed to the weight and she noticed it no more than the weight of her clothes.

She was not the first in the waiting-room, but she was called first, and the tests were done quickly, and she was out by half past nine—enough time to go home first. She walked out into the sunshine feeling buoyant. She had had another reasonable night's sleep last night, and Gerry had again popped in a couple of times. He said three times, so perhaps she was actually sleeping during one of them. How could a young healthy boy like that manage to wake up? She was amazed and touched. Also by his endeavours on her behalf. He had gone through the register again for Thoday-Walken babies and had found one born in nineteen fifty which gave the rank or profession of father as Master Butcher and the address as 5 Petunia Street, East Acton. He was going there today to see if he could find anything out.

She went into the tube station and bought her ticket and as she turned away from the ticket booth she saw Jim Blackburn coming towards her. Oh fuck, she thought, that's the last thing I need, a row with Jim. His face was set sternly, and she braced herself, seeing there was nowhere that she could hide; but to her astonishment he walked straight past her, his eyes simply not registering her. She was so surprised that she turned to look after him, forgetting for the moment that she ought to be glad to be ignored. He went to the back of the queue she had just left. Her staring must have caught his eye, and he turned and looked, and his eye brushed over her without recognition, and she managed to remember to withdraw her gaze before it became obvious to him that he ought to know her. She walked slowly away, feeling dazed, and by automatic reaction went down the stairs to get her train.

There was no doubt about it, he had not recognized her. It was impossible to look at someone you knew as if you didn't know them. So what did that mean? That she had changed, physically, so much that a person who had known her for years, who had been her lover even, did not recognize her? Another moment and he would have seen her trumpet case and then perhaps things would have been different. She wished she had gone and spoken to him. Too late now, anyway. Gerry was gone when she got home. She telephoned the doctor and made an appointment for the following week, picked up the car and drove off to her session. She was thoughtful all through it. The rest of the orchestra, seeing her virtually every day, seemed to have no trouble with her, but Jim hadn't seen her for a long time. They had only commented on her hair, which was the obvious change. And Malcolm had said only that morning,

'You're looking a bit better today, Aggie. Bit

of colour in your cheeks. And you're putting on weight, I see.'

'You see more than I do,' she said.

'Ah, gypsy Petulengro sees all. But I'm glad you're not looking quite so bloody awful. I was getting worried about you.'

'I know you were, Malc. I can tell you know. It's the way you keep sticking a thermometer into my mouth during rests.'

'What's he keep sticking in your mouth?' Bill asked across them, and the conversation had degenerated in the usual way.

They broke at two, and they were not on again until four-thirty, so she rang Polly for the latest bulletin, and found her much happier too.

'Everything's fine,' she said. 'In fact, everything's better than that. It's all right, Ag. Last night we had it all out, and I had a really serious talk with him, and the upshot is—oh Ag, he asked me to marry him.'

'And did you say yes?' she asked, hiding her astonishment as well as possible.

'Sort of. I mean, he didn't really ask me yes or no. He said, "I suppose we had better think about getting married," and I just sort of agreed. But the main thing is, he agrees with me about Janice, that it isn't fair on her, if she really is much keener on him than he is on her, to let her go on thinking he's hers exclusively. I told him it was far crueller than telling her the truth, and he agreed with me, and he said he'd not done it before out of sheer cowardice, but that now he was definitely going to tell her about me and tell her it was all over with her.'

'When?'

'When what?'

'When is he going to tell her?'

'He didn't say exactly when.'

'And you let him get away with that?'

'It's not a case of getting away with it,' she said irritably. 'I did press him at first, but he said he had to choose the right moment.'

'Oh yeah!'

'No, come on, Ag, he really did mean it. He was quite sincere. I *know* when he's telling the truth and he was telling the truth then.' No answer to that. 'He has to choose the right moment, and that's fair enough. I mean if she's going to be upset—'

Quite. If she's going to be upset then it doesn't matter what moment he does it. But there was no point in telling Polly that. There was a limit to the amount of truth that will mix with wilful self-deception without causing an explosion. When you had being in love in the crucible you had to add truth drop by drop from a pipette with great caution. Agatha held her tongue, and told instead her own news, and Gerry's progress.

'I think that's terrific. He's a good kid, isn't he?'

'And all done for love,' Agatha said drily. 'Talking of which I saw his father this morning.'

'Christ. What did he say?'

'That's the odd thing. He didn't recognize me. Walked straight past me.'

'Oh I've done that hundreds of times. It's terribly embarrassing afterwards.'

'Yes, I suppose so,' Agatha said thoughtfully. Well, probably Polly was right. There was nothing in it after all.

* * *

Gerry was elated when she got home.

'I really think I've got her this time,' he said eagerly.

'All right, let me get my shoes off and sit down, and you can tell me All.'

'Had a hard day?' he said sympathetically.

'Oh not so bad. More boring than hard. I don't like recording sessions. All that sitting around. Now then, what have you got to tell me?'

'Well, I went to East Acton this morning, and found the house all right, but there was no one in. I was very disappointed—somehow it never occurred to me that they wouldn't be there, but I suppose it would be more likely to be that way than otherwise. I mean, people ought to be at work, oughtn't they. Well, I was standing about on the path looking lost, wondering what to do next, when the door of the next-door house opened and this young woman came out with a kid in a pushchair. You see, the houses are little semi-detacheds, and the doors are together in the middle of the house with just a little low privet hedge between them.'

Agatha nodded. 'I know what you mean.'

'Anyway when she saw me she gave a what-do-you-want sort of smile, so I smiled back politely and she said did I want anything so I said I was looking for Mrs Walken who used to live there, and did she know if Mrs Walken still lived there and she shook her head and said no it was the Andersons lived there, and she looked just a fraction suspicious and I said that I had that address for the Walkens but that it was 1950 and I supposed they'd moved but I'd come along in hope because it was very important I traced them.'

'Did she know them?'

'No. I hoped she'd pick up the bait and she did—she said she'd only been living there for five years, but that the people on the other side had been there for much longer and maybe they'd know. So I thanked her and went and tried the house on the other side—number three.'

'And there was no one in?' she hazarded. He took on a very smug expression.

'Wrong. There was the woman in, *and* she knew the Walkens. And she said they'd moved about eight years ago when Albert Walken retired. And I asked her if she knew their address. She looked a bit suspicious then, so I told her why I wanted to know—not all the details of course,' he added hastily when Agatha's mouth opened to protest.

'And did she give it to you?'

'No. She said she didn't know their address. I suppose she hadn't been that friendly with them.'

'Oh for God's sake,' Agatha said, 'Stop building me up and letting me down. I feel like a yo-yo.'

Gerry grinned impishly. 'All right, I'll give it to you straight. She didn't know their address, but she did know that they'd gone to live in a cottage in the country, in a little village in Norfolk, near Norwich, called Rockland St Mary. So I went to Trafalgar Square to that post office where they have directories for the whole country and I looked up the Norwich one, and I found one Walken, E. Walken, and I've got the address and the telephone number and all you have to do is ring her up and make an appointment to go and see her. I think,' he added pompously, 'that it's beyond the bounds of possibility that there would be two Walkens living in one remote village in Norfolk.'

Agatha stared at him thoughtfully. 'I wonder why Norfolk? Except that Thoday is a Norfolk name, maybe that's where she came from, and she wanted to go back there.' She shivered with excitement. 'I wonder if she really is the one who knew my mother? And how well she knew her. Gerry, you've done a terrific job. I don't know how to thank you.'

He came quickly across to her, knelt on the floor by her chair, and said,

'Yes you do. You know I only do it because I love you.'

'Don't,' she said. 'Please don't. You don't love me—I'm far too old for that.'

He shook his head irritably. 'Why do you go on about age? Do you think I'm too young to know what love is? Do you think love is the province of the over-thirties?'

'No,' she said slowly, sadly. 'I think love is a thing we begin to forget far too quickly. The over-thirties I know love very little.'

'Well then, why bring age into it?'

'I suppose because I know you will change your mind about this. In a little while—a few months perhaps—maybe a few years,' she added seeing his objection ready–formed, 'you will feel quite differently about me.'

'But what does that prove? Why should you think a thing can't be love unless it stays the same for ever?'

It was a new thought. She stared into his eyes, pierced by his young beauty, and said,

'I don't know. I suppose we are brought up to think in terms of duration. You are right, of course, it doesn't make a thing invalid that it will not be the same for ever.'

'Well then.'

'Gerry, I don't think I can give you what you

want,' she said. He looked at her solemnly.

'I know what you mean,' he said. 'You can't give me everything I want, perhaps. But you could at least let me love you.'

She sighed, and held her arms out to him, and he put his own arms round her, and rested his head on her shoulder, his cheek against hers.

'Yes, I can do that. It's the least I can do,' she said, stroking his head. 'I just don't want to make you unhappy.' Even as she said it, she chided herself. Where have you heard those words before? she asked herself.

'Don't worry,' he said into her ear. 'You can't make me unhappy. That's up to me.'

He was very clear-headed, she thought. Much more so than she was about such things. Perhaps that was the generation gap; perhaps today's youngsters, being brought up with fewer illusions and more reality, had a better chance of grasping the nettle of happiness firmly enough to avoid being stung. It was too late for her and her generation; but for him there might still be a chance. The inconsequential thought went through her head that it was fortunate she had been taken off the pill, or she would have been very tempted to give him the rest of what he wanted and let him screw her. Saved by the pill! and in her case, from a death worse than fate.

* * *

Mrs Walken, when Agatha got through to her on Saturday, did not seem to be surprised to be contacted by Agatha Shaw's daughter. Agatha had been afraid that she would be too old to be much help, perhaps going simple, but she sounded quite young and would have sounded brisk if it had not been for her strong Norfolk accent. When Agatha asked if she could come and see her to ask her about her mother she seemed, not precisely reluctant, but hesitant, but she said in the end,

'Well, yes, all right, if you think there's anything I can tell you.'

'You must know more about her than I do,' Agatha said. 'When may I come?'

'It'll have to be at a weekend, because I work during the week. Just the school dinners, but it keeps me busy.'

'What about next Saturday then? Saturday about lunchtime?'

'All right.'

'And, one other thing—do you have any photographs of my mother?'

'Well I don't know,' she said doubtfully. 'I might have. I'll have a look for you.'

'All fixed,' she told Gerry when she had rung off. 'Next Saturday. I'm not working, so I can drive up in the morning and back in the afternoon. I don't know how long it will take. I'll have to start off pretty early, I suppose.'

'Can I come with you?'

'Of course, if you want. I don't suppose she'll mind. She sounded all right—quite compos mentis I mean. But I wonder why she wasn't surprised to hear from me? She didn't say anything like "Fancy, after all these years" or anything.'

'Some people,' Gerry said, with wisdom beyond his years, 'are never surprised by anything.'

* * *

Wednesday morning brought the new appointment with the doctor. She looked at Agatha this time as if she saw her, and Agatha found it alarming to discover herself suddenly visible. What could the hospital report have said?

'How have you been feeling?'

'All right, I suppose,' Agatha made the automatic reply, and then realizing how stupid that was, added, 'I've been feeling very tired. Especially in the mornings.'

'Any dizziness? Feeling of pressure in the ears? Spots before the eyes?'

'Dizziness, yes. I fainted once. And I've been having trouble with my eyes.'

'Mm.' The doctor appeared rather gratified than otherwise by these revelations. 'I'm not surprised. Your blood pressure is very low and you seem to be rather anaemic.'

'Oh.' Agatha was rather taken aback by the

discovery that there was something physically wrong with her. She had braced herself to argue the toss, and the toss was tossed back into her hands. 'Could that cause—well, hallucinations?'

Now the doctor was wrong-footed. 'Hallucinations? I'm not sure what you mean.'

'Oh. Nothing really,' Agatha backed down hastily. 'Nightmares, I suppose. I sleep very badly.'

'Restlessness at night could certainly be caused by anaemia. I'm going to prescribe you a course of iron tablets, and I'd like you to pay attention to your diet and make sure you get some red meat, particularly liver. Now, how have your periods been? When was the last one?'

Agatha screwed up her face in thought. 'Actually, I think I've missed one. I know I had one when I was down in Bristol—when was that? Hang on, I'll look in my diary.' She thumbed through her engagements diary. 'Yes, it was July the 4th it came on.'

'And you haven't had one since?' Agatha shook her head, working, like the doctor, through a calender. 'You have missed one then. But that's not unusual, since you've come off the pill. It sometimes takes your body a while to readjust.'

'Did anything show up on the tests? I wondered why I had to go back and do them again.'

'Well there were some rather strange readings on the hormonal tests, which was why we wanted them done again. And in fact on the second test the readings came up quite different, more or less normal, so we think there must have been some error the first time.'

'So there's nothing wrong with me?'

'Nothing serious. You're obviously a little run down, anaemic, probably underweight. I want you to make sure you eat regular, balanced meals, get as much fresh air and gentle exercise as possible, and try not to worry. You'll find you sleep better as your physical condition improves. And stay off the pill a little longer, if you will. I'd like you to have a rest from that for a few months. Do you want me to prescribe some alternative form—'

'No, thank you. If I ever do need it, I'll sort it out for myself.' Agatha hesitated. What about the rest of it, the shrinking, the hair and eyes, the haunting or dream, whichever it was? Could she bring it up? Should she bring it up? If she imagined something as wildly impossible as copulating with a ghost, could not the other things be imagination? And yet Polly said she had shrunk; and her hair had definitely changed colour. Was that imagination? While she hesitated, the doctor said,

'Now is there anything else you want to ask me? Anything I can help you with?'

'What about my hair going blonde?' Agatha asked abruptly. The doctor frowned.

'Frankly, I don't know. But changes of hair colour are common, though it generally happens more gradually. I don't know what could have caused such an acceleration in your case, but as there doesn't seem to be anything seriously wrong with you, I shouldn't worry about it.'

'And my eyes? They've gone almost completely brown.'

'Again, the same thing.'

'But you said you got strange readings the first time. Couldn't that have had something to do with it?'

The doctor looked harried. 'If your body had undergone a drastic hormonal change, it could have many incalculable effects. But my own belief is that some impurity got into the test material, because it is unlikely that the readings could have reverted to normal so quickly.'

'But if it was a rapid, temporary aberration—?'

'Even if it was, as it has been, as you say, temporary. I don't think there is anything to worry about. But I'd like you to come and see me again in two weeks, and if you are still worried then, we can do the tests again. It is important for you not to worry, to avoid stress. I can give you another prescription for some valium—'

Agatha made up her mind. 'Doctor, will you look at these?' From her bag she pulled out the mugshots she had had taken after her last visit. 'I took these photographs in a booth after I last saw you—about a month ago.'

'July the 16th,' the doctor said, glancing at the card.

'Look at them, and look at me. Don't you see how I've changed?'

The doctor compared with an appearance of care. 'No, I can't say I do. These photographs are notoriously unlike the subject. You should see my passport photos—my own mother wouldn't know me.'

An unhappy choice of phrase. 'I am smaller than I was. My best friend remarked on it. And whatever you say about the photographs, I can see how my face is changing.'

The doctor looked at her kindly. 'My dear, you mustn't let these things prey on your mind. These photographs show nothing except that they're poor photographs—and we all have strange ideas about what we look like. Your hair changing colour has obviously upset you, and has made you think you look different, and of course hair colour does make a difference to appearance, otherwise why would so many of us tint it? But as to your features changing—you know that isn't possible.'

Agatha felt defeated. Another minute and she would hear the word imagination.

'And the fact that I'm smaller?'

'That, I'm afraid, is your imagination.'

'Is it imagination that my clothes are all too

big for me?'

'But you would expect that if you've lost weight,' the doctor said with such sweet reasonableness that for a moment Agatha thought she must be right. At any rate, there was no point in arguing. The terrible thing was that once anything threw doubt on the nature of reality, the whole fabric began to disintegrate. What was to prove that she was not imagining this entire interview in the doctor's surgery? Wearily she put the photographs back into her bag and prepared to leave.

'Wait just a minute for your prescription,' the doctor arrested her, and scribbled it out. 'Here we are. Take the full course, and remember what I said about diet and fresh air. And I'll see you again in two weeks. And above all, try not to worry.'

She would have had to be blind to miss the irony in Agatha's farewell smile.

CHAPTER TEN

It rained all the way to Norfolk, and what with the road conditions and the usual bloody Saturday drivers who insisted on doing twenty-five right smack in the middle of the road, it was gone one o'clock by the time they drove into Rockland St Mary. On the credit side, the rain stopped and the sun came out while they were asking their way to Rose Cottage, and by the time they were walking up the immensely long concrete path which ran between well-tended ranks of vegetables, everything that wasn't sparkling was steaming. The cottage looked like a child's drawing, oblong-faced with evenly disposed windows and a door smack in the middle, a flat and characterless little place, apart from the size and neatness of the garden.

'She must be active, if she does all this,' Gerry observed. 'I presume Albert's passed on, if the telephone's registered in her name.'

'I hadn't thought of that,' she said, gaping at him admiringly. 'Aren't you clever.'

He smirked. 'Oh, just my usual methods, doctor.'

'Don't mention doctors to me. Hush—here she is.'

The door opened, and Mrs Walken blinked against the strong sunlight, looking from one to the other of them questioningly. She was small and slight and as nondescript as her house, an elderly woman with a grey perm and glasses with coloured frames, a lined face, and a shapeless body tucked into a neat flower-patterned dress that bore the unmistakable style of St Michael.

'Hello,' Agatha said, smiling as winningly as possible. 'I'm Agatha Shaw, and this is my friend Gerry Blackburn, who's been helping me find out about my mother. It was he who managed to trace you, Mrs Walken.'

She looked at Gerry in a markedly unfriendly way, and then stood back, holding the door open in what appeared to be very grudging hospitality.

'You'd better come in. Mind the step, it's a bit uneven. And you,' to Gerry, 'had better mind your head on the doors. They're not built for giants.'

Agatha stepped over the threshold, and after the strong sunlight it seemed very dark. Sparks shot up before her eyes as she groped forward. The house was cool and smelled clean and dusty and—there was a scenty sort of smell too that she could not at once place, but she suddenly felt a very strong sensation of déja-vu. A thud and a muted cry from behind her told her that Gerry had discovered for himself the vertical dimensions of the doorway. She turned her head to smile at him; the sunlight flooding in through the open door was dazzling, and he was cut out black and indistinguishable against the frame of white light. And the smell she realized was apples. The coloured sparks flashed brighter with the sensation of pressure in her ears, and she felt herself reeling forward and down in what seemed like slow motion as dizziness overcame her

down down into the dark falling spread like a star the smell of apples and the dark shape in the door of the barn the boy and the smell of apples going down into the dark forever because it was all over for her

despair

swinging, swinging, and the pressure growing pressure in her head and the smell of apples overpowering pressure bursting down into the dark

black

for ever.

She came up slowly to discover herself lying on the sofa in a tight, low-ceilinged chintzy room whose small windows were bright white oblongs cut out against the dark. She felt nauseous, and choked. Gerry was kneeling beside her holding her hands, which were icy cold, and Mrs Walken was standing a little way off with an air of dissociating herself almost violently from the situation.

'Are you all right?' Gerry was saying anxiously.

'Yes, I think so. I was just dizzy. Did I faint?'

'Right out. I only just caught you. What's up?'

'I don't know. Just the strain of driving, I expect. I'm all right now. I felt a bit sick, but it's passing off.'

She pushed him gently away and swung herself upright into a sitting position. She looked at Mrs Walken. 'I'm sorry—making a fool of myself. I've been a bit run down recently, and I get dizzy. I think it was the darkness after the strong light.'

'Well, as long as you're all right,' the woman said doubtfully. 'Do you want a drink of water?'

'No thank you.' Why did people offer you water? Now tea, or even coffee—but they obviously weren't going to be offered anything. For some reason they were unwelcome. Mrs Walken had the air of one determined to do her duty however unpleasant it was.

'Well you'd better sit down,' she said to Gerry, and when he had placed himself upon the sofa, she sat down herself on an overstuffed chair opposite them. 'So you're Agatha Shaw's daughter? I must say you don't look a bit like her. The last time I saw you you were a new-born babe, and covered in plaster dust.'

'You actually saw me being pulled out of the ruin then?'

'Oh yes, I was there. That was how I was able to identify Annie—'

'Annie?'

'She didn't like to be called Agatha. I always knew her as Annie. Annie and Nellie, that was us. Like a double-act.'

'Sorry, I interrupted. You were saying about identifying the body?'

'They say she saved your life at the expense of her own, though strictly speaking she should have gone down to the shelter, but towards the end of the war the raids were going on all the time practically, and you couldn't spend your whole life down there. Anyway, they didn't smell too nice, and they were crowded and stuffy. And of course she might not have been able to move. You were only a couple of days old, so she might have been still bedridden. In those days we didn't use to get up right away after birth the way they do now.'

'So she was in bed at the time?'

'So it seems. She was in her nightie anyway, and you were as naked as the palm of my hand.' She glanced suspiciously at Gerry to see if he would make anything of that, but he was being politely and intelligently interested, and she looked back at Agatha. That faint expression of distaste came into her face again, as she said, 'I identified her by her belongings. As to recognizing her face, her own mother wouldn't have known her, always supposing she'd had a mother which she didn't.'

Agatha drew her breath with difficulty. 'She'd changed then? I mean, her features?'

'Changed?' Mrs Walken looked fractionally puzzled, but she went on with a kind of brutal relish. 'You could say so. She didn't have any features to speak of. All smashed to pulp they were, and her hair had gone quite white. Horrible it was. And she'd been so pretty when she was younger.'

'You knew her as a girl, then?'

'We went to school together. I was born and bred in these parts—that's why we came back here when Albert retired, though he was a Londoner. But his health wasn't good, and if I was going to be left a widow I wanted to be in my own place. Well he's gone now, and here I am, and I can't say I miss him much. Men are a trial and a nuisance when all's said and done, but I suppose we have to have 'em. Is he your young man?' She asked abruptly and with obvious disapproval. Agatha guessed this was the source of annoyance, that she felt Gerry was too young to be her boy-friend. Agatha smiled depreciatingly.

'Oh no, good heavens no. He's the son of a friend of mine. He's been helping me with my search while he's on holiday from school.'

'Oh. Well I'm sorry,' Mrs Walken said shortly, and turned her gaze away from the offending young man. 'Where was I? Oh yes—I was born in Rockland, but when I was ten my dad moved down to Suffolk, to Southwold, and I went to school there, and that's where I met your mother.'

'She lived in Southwold?'

'Don't you know anything about her?' Mrs Walken seemed surprised.

'Nothing at all. There was no one to tell me. At the orphanage they weren't even sure of my date of birth.'

'Well your mother was an orphanage child too. There was a big place in Southwold then, Marsh House it was called, and they all went to the village school with the rest of us. She was a pretty little thing, very bright and lively, and long dark ringlets. I always remember that, because my hair wouldn't curl and I had it pinched and singed by my mother twice a week to try and make it curl, and did it make my eyes water! But never the sign of a curl, and there was Annie with her long ringlets. But she was such a lively girl, you had to like her. We took to each other right away.'

'So she was an orphan—did she have any relatives?'

'Not that I ever heard. I don't know how she came to be orphaned. I never asked. Well anyway, we were at school until we were fifteen, both being bright girls and we took our matriculation, and then of course we had to think about getting some work. Times were hard then—'

'When would that be?' Agatha interposed. All this seemed so strange to her, a fairy tale about imaginary figures, and yet it was part of her, it was her own mother, whose flesh had made her, who had, if Mrs E. Walken, Nellie Thoday that was, was right, given her life that she might live. She felt weirdly ambivalent, as if she were splitting into two.

'That would be 1929, in the summer. There wasn't much work around at the time, not for anyone. My mother wanted me to go into service, and I dare say I should have, only Annie didn't like that idea. She was a very bright girl, as I've said, and she didn't like the idea of being a servant. She wanted her freedom, like, and she was set on working in a factory. So she said to me, Nellie, she said, why don't we both go and get jobs in Lowestoft, and that way your mother won't worry so much. Well I liked the idea, and Annie came and talked my mother round, and so that's what we did. She could have talked anyone into anything could Annie, in those days.'

Her face had softened a little at the memory, and Agatha had a sudden vivid picture of little mousy Nellie with her obstinately straight hair being dominated by, and adoring, the vivacious, pretty Annie, with her dark curls and blue eyes and rosy cheeks; adoring her, and following her as a faithful lieutenant, sometimes perhaps a little sullen and jealous, but always obedient, always loyal. Did that picture come from this plain woman's words alone, or was it possible to inherit a memory? Or was it, dread word again, just imagination?

'And did you go and live in Lowestoft?'

'Not at first, no. Girls didn't live away from home in those days. We got jobs in the factory—not on the lines, you understand, but in the office. Annie was a book-keeper, and I was a clerk. We used to go in every day on the bus, and come home the same way. But when we were both seventeen, Annie wanted to go and get lodgings in the town.'

'Had she been living at the orphanage all

that time?'

'Oh no, they didn't let them stay on after fifteen. She'd had lodgings in Southwold, you see, so it was sense for her to go nearer to her work. Mum wasn't happy about it—she thought we'd get into trouble—but Dad was always for us getting on and being independent. And Annie talked them round anyway. Dad said as long as I was with Annie I should be all right, and when Mum had seen the place and talked to the landlady she felt better about it. Annie found the place—she did everything—and a lovely place it was, as they went in those days. A big house on London Road—you could have seen the sea from the attic windows, only we had the first floor back, a nice big room if a bit dark, and all our meals, and the landlady, Mrs Holloway, she couldn't have been nicer if she was our own mother. Annie used to say it was the first mother she'd ever had, and Mrs Holloway wouldn't have heard a word against Annie. Mad about her, she was. But then, everyone took to Annie.'

'Did she have boy-friends?'

Mrs Walken looked disapproving, the softness of her face sliding away like a lizard down a crack as she came back to the present. 'No, never. Not then. Of course all the young men were mad for her, and they were always chasing her, but she didn't want anything to do with them. She laughed at them, and it drove them mad. She thought they were silly. Nellie, she'd say, tossing her head, I don't ever want to get married. She liked her freedom, you see. She'd say, Nellie, let's be old maids together, and have a lot of fun. But it wasn't fun like youngsters mean it today,' she added forbiddingly.

'I'm sure not,' Agatha murmured. With every word, the picture in her head grew stronger, of the leader and the led, the strong-headed young woman and the adoring dog-like lieutenant. But what went wrong? There was bitterness in this woman, a hardness that seemed to stem from some bad disappointment somewhere along the line.

'So how long did you work in the factory?' she asked in a prompting kind of way. Gerry was very quiet—she glanced sideways and saw that he was effacing himself as far as possible. So he had felt the hostility too?

'It must have been about five years altogether. We were happy there too, until the last year, when the dreams started.'

Agatha and Gerry both flinched simultaneously. 'Dreams?' she asked, trying to sound casually interested, and to her own ears at least failing miserably. Mrs Walken looked from one to the other.

'Nightmares,' she said shortly. 'You wouldn't think a little ole dream could make such a difference to a person, but I tell you after those nightmares she was a different person. She changed—to me and to herself. She wasn't the same.'

By the tone of her voice, this was where the bitterness began. She changed. It sounded to Agatha like ordinary, plain old jealousy, so common, and so painful. The inference was there to be drawn. We were happy together, wanted no one else, until she changed. But the dreams? The nightmares? Agatha discovered she was trembling, and had to make a great effort to control herself.

'Can you tell me about the dreams? Did she tell you about them?'

'Oh yes, she told me,' sourly. 'In the end I'd have been glad not to hear. But then—' She glanced again at Gerry. 'This isn't for his ears, you know. I don't mind telling you, because you're her daughter, but what's he to her?'

Gerry and Agatha exchanged a glance. Agatha considered for a moment arguing the point, but the woman was so hostile that she decided very quickly not to. 'Gerry, would you mind awfully—?'

He took the hint, bless him, though she could see his face was red with repressed anger and frustration. With a look she promised to tell him everything.

'I'll wait outside,' he said. 'You don't mind if I look round your garden, do you?'

'Suit yourself,' she said indifferently. When he had gone, it took the old woman a while to recapture her thread, and Agatha waited patiently, knowing better than to try to hurry her.

'It started off,' she said at last, 'with just bad dreams. Annie would wake up crying and shouting, and I'd have to quiet her. She didn't remember what the nightmares were about, and as soon as I'd quieted her down, she'd go off back to sleep. But they started to get more frequent—at least once a week, sometimes more, and she'd be harder to calm down. Sometimes she let out such a scream that she'd wake the house, and Mrs Holloway would come up, and there were some complaints from the other lodgers, though I will say that Mrs Holloway wouldn't have it, and told them they should be ashamed to make a fuss.'

'But the dreams grew worse?'

'Oh yes, they got worse all right. And it started to get her down, her health and everything. She lost that lovely healthy look she'd always had. She got pale and peaky and nervous—you've never seen such a change in a girl. She'd always been so lively and full of fun, and she got so's she'd jump if you slammed a door. And she was afraid to go to sleep, because of the dreams, and she'd sit up to all hours, reading until her eyes were ruined, so as not to go to sleep. But of course in the end she'd have to go to sleep, and then the nightmares would come. Terrible it was. To hear her screaming and crying—' The fists clenched, and Agatha saw small mousy Nellie's fury on behalf of her idol, and the frustration of not being able to help.

'Well of course her work suffered too, and she was making mistakes, and you can't make mistakes at book-keeping. They were very nice about it at the factory, and kept her on long after any other firm would have given her the push. But in the end they had to get rid of her, so then she had no work either, and that didn't help. We managed somehow, but her health was cracking up, and it couldn't go on.'

'Did she tell you what the dreams were about?'

Mrs Walken gave her a curious look, of speculation and hesitation. 'She did, but not until the end; she always said before that she didn't remember, though to my mind she remembered well enough but didn't want to talk about it. And when she did tell me, I could see why.' She paused again, as if wondering whether to tell, and Agatha leaned forward a fraction to encourage her. 'She said,' she told it with slow relish, 'that she dreamed about a man—that she was—that she was being raped by a man.'

'That does sound like a nightmare,' Agatha said, and the fact that she was shaken sounded so clearly in her voice that Mrs Walken was mollified.

'You might say so. What that girl went through was terrible, night after night, afraid to go to sleep because as soon as she did *he* would come and start doing *that* to her. But what really finished her was that in the end she said she started to enjoy it. Well, you may be shocked—I can tell you I was—but neither you nor me was as shocked as Annie was with herself. She hated herself for it. I kept telling her she couldn't help what was in her dreams, but she said that it must be something bad in *her* that was just coming out through her dreams, and nothing I could say would change her mind about it. That was what was killing her, you see, thinking that she was wicked deep down and didn't know about it.'

Agatha said nothing. She was very still, and the words seemed to fall about her like cold heavy drops, like mercury, joining and parting senselessly, poisoning. Her mouth was dry, and she could not have spoken if she wanted. In the end Nellie went on without prompting, and the emotion was gone from her voice, as if after that time she had felt nothing so deeply again. The ruin of her friend had ended her emotional life.

'It couldn't go on as it was, of course, but even I was shocked when she told me she was going into a convent. But that's what she did. She wanted to purify herself, you see, of what she thought of as the evil in her. She went in, that would be in 1934, and she took her orders in 1935, and what peace she found there I do not know, because she never wrote to me in all that time. I only hope she found some peace, poor creature.'

'And was that the last you saw of her?' Agatha asked at last. 'Until her death, I mean?'

Mrs Walken looked at her strangely. 'It's shaken you, hasn't it? Well, I suppose it's to your credit that you can feel it. No, I saw her again, in 1940 it was. I went to London to work in a munitions factory just after the war started, and so I thought I'd get in contact with her. She was in a convent in Ladbroke Grove, the Little Sisters of the Poor I think they called it. I went there to see if I could see her, and they told me that she'd come out, given up her orders and just left. They gave me her address, and I went round to see her.' Her eyes grew distant again. 'Well, I've never seen such a change in a person. I wouldn't have known her, except that she knew me. She looked years older, and her hair—well I suppose it was with having it shaved in the convent, but all those lovely glossy curls were gone, and her hair was just like straw. And—' the bitterness came out again, and Agatha guessed here was the heart of the matter, 'and, she'd got married.'

'Married?'

'Straight after she came out. Of course, that may be why she came out, I don't know, because I didn't ask her much about it. I didn't like him. He was a soldier, of course, and away most of the time, but I saw him once or twice when he came home on leave. Nasty piece of work, I'd call him. I suppose she saw something in him. She said she'd met him when he was just called up, and married him because he was going away to war, and might be killed. Didn't seem too much of a reason to me. I asked her if she still had the dreams, and she laughed in a funny sort of way and said she wasn't bothered by them any more, and you could take that any way you liked. She was changed, I tell you. I was only living round the corner from her, but I didn't see all that much of her, because somehow or other she wasn't the Annie I'd known. She was sort of coarsened. Of course, she was working as a clippie, and that would do it, even if being married to that man didn't do it.'

'You didn't like him then.'

'He was a man, and when you get down to it they're all the same. Animals, nasty brutish animals. Mind you, my husband wasn't as bad as some—he was older, and he'd been wounded in the war when I met him—after your mother was dead that was—so he'd been gentled, you might say. But he was still a man, there was no getting away from it.'

'And what was his name?'

'Who?' Mrs Walken looked puzzled. 'My husband?'

'No, my father.'

She snorted derisively. 'You're as wise as I am about that. Though if you mean Annie's husband, I can tell you that. It was Bill Mason.

But as to your father's name—Bill Mason was sent to France in August 1943, and you were a few days old when Annie was killed in September 1944, so you can work it out for yourself.'

Agatha stared, and Mrs Walken's mouth twisted with bitter contempt.

'Why do you think he left her anyway? He came back on leave in March and she was pregnant. If he hadn't been killed as soon as he got back to France he'd have divorced her.' She looked away, and Agatha could see the betrayal still hurt, after all these years. 'I wasn't sorry when that doodlebug fell on her house, and she was brought out smashed all to bits. I was only sorry that you were got out alive.'

The harsh voice stopped, and in the room there was no sound but the ticking of the clock and no movement but the dust drifting down through the bars of sunlight.

CHAPTER ELEVEN

'Do you want me to drive?' Gerry said. It snapped her out of it.

'No of course not. I'm all right.'

'You look pale. I expect you're hungry. Shall we have something to eat before we go back? We don't want you fainting at the wheel.'

'All right. We'll stop at a pub and get some

bread and cheese. They're still open.'

Over a ploughman's lunch she told Gerry all he had not heard. He was very quiet afterwards, and Agatha guessed he was trying out all the possible alternative theories in his head, just as she had. But all he said was,

'Did you show her the photograph?'

'She said she didn't recognize it.'

'Do you think she was telling the truth?'

'I don't see why she would lie.'

'No, nor do I.'

Not until they were half way home did he bring up the subject of the dreams.

'A real ghost then, do you think? The same one?'

Agatha did not look at him. 'She said nothing about ghosts. She talked about dreams.'

'True, but she only knew what she was told.'

'So do we.'

'Can a dream be dreamed by two people who have never communicated with each other?'

'Who the hell knows?' Agatha said irritably. 'Race memory seems to exist. Who knows what the mind is capable of.'

'But a ghost seems more likely, doesn't it?'

Now she glanced, half-amused, half-exasperated. 'You'd like it to be a ghost?'

'Well, wouldn't you? Sooner than have to think you're going crazy?'

She breathed hard. 'Some nails are better

not hit on the head.'

'Do you dream he's—he's—'

'Raping me?'

'Well—'

'No,' she said, and felt him relax for a second before she said, 'It isn't *rape*.'

'Oh God, Agatha—' She knew he wanted to touch her, and she said quickly,

'Please don't. I'm on the brink of shattering into tiny little pieces, and if you touch me or sympathize with me I don't know what will happen.'

There was silence for some time, and then Agatha said.

'We aren't very much further forward. We still don't know why *her*, why *me*. If it is haunting it can't be random. And if it isn't—'

'Yes?'

'Oh God, I don't know. Nothing makes sense. I may be going crazy, but even that doesn't explain everything. In fact, that doesn't explain anything. The worst thing is not knowing.'

'We must find out more. Perhaps we can find some of the nuns who were at the convent with her. She may have told them more than she'd tell that woman. Or—'

'Or what?' He was silent. 'Well?'

'Agatha, if it is a ghost, couldn't you communicate with it, find out what it wants?'

'If I knew how to do that, don't you think I would have tried it?'

'We could try the Ouija board again,' he said in a small voice. Her knuckles whitened on the steering wheel.

'I am so afraid,' she whispered. 'I keep asking myself, what is going to happen next? But if I knew, maybe that would be worse.'

'How could it be worse?'

Her eyes flickered whitely sideways at him. 'If someone said they would tell you the day of your death, would you want to know?'

* * *

There was work, that was a constant. She took on every engagement she could fit in, even some out-of-town dates that were hardly worth her while—anything to keep busy. The dream came once or twice a week now, and there seemed to be a sort of equilibrium struck; she did not yield more, and he did not press her less; she woke still in the morning feeling exhausted and used up, was often faint and dizzy when she rose from her bed, sometimes was even nauseous. But Nellie Walken's story had given her some resistance, at least to the sense of shame. Whatever it was that was working on her would not get her that way.

It was not exactly that things were easier, but she had taken up the strain now, and could hold on. In the mornings she would look at her bleached face, the dark and shadowed eyes like holes cut in a piece of paper that were unnervingly not her own eyes, and would see the taut lines harden. *I can hold on*, she would think, *for one more day*. And then one more. Taking one day at a time, as alcoholics were told. She could not and would not think of the future. The face in the mirror, worn and strained, still retained a glimmer of humour, though it did not reside in those eyes. *Possessed*, the word came to her. Not devil-possession—he was not the devil, that man, whatever else he was; what came from him was need, want, not evil. He wanted her, but she did not know why. He wanted from her what other men had wanted before, and it had not hurt her to give it; or at least, she had not been aware of the hurt. But what he took from her was hard to replace, and day by day she was being worn out. But she could hold on, she could hold on, though her soul was being stretched thinner and thinner.

Only the music replenished anything in her; sometimes after a concert she would feel eased, and Malcolm would smile at her with that particular intimate smile he had when they had played particularly well together; when their two sounds had twined like the strands of a rope, like the supporting strands of a spider's web from which the net of the music swung delicate and strong and shimmering. He would smile at her, and sometimes put his arms round her and lavish his rough endearment on her, but it was the sense of his soul leaning against hers that helped her. The hands on her body were so remote that it might have been someone else's flesh he touched.

She had gone beyond finding any help in Gerry, too, and as if he understood that he kept away from her when she was home, even went so far as to get himself a job to tide him over until he went up to Oxford. She was glad in a distant way; her struggle took up all her energy, and seemed to be all her own. He could not help her, and she could not give him anything. When she did see him, she spoke cheerfully of her improvement—she had put on a little weight, and her appetite had improved, though she suffered from bouts of indigestion—and avoided meeting his eyes. She did not want to see in them how he found her changed from day to day.

Because she knew that the equilibrium could not last. It was only a respite, a resting place where she could catch her breath for a moment before the real struggle came. And whatever explanation she tried to attach to what was happening to her, she could not see that it could have any ending but her destruction: or what was it all for? All she could hope for was that she would understand before she went down what it was that had happened to her. She felt that she had always known she was doomed, that only joy could ever have surprised her.

* * *

'Oh Ag, how have you been? It's ages since I saw you.'

'I'm all right. You sound happy. I concluded things must have been going all right for you. How's Brian treating you?'

'Oh, everything's wonderful. I've moved in with him now. Well, there didn't seem any point in keeping two places going when I was spending practically every night here anyway.'

'And Janice has disappeared from the scene, has she?'

'Oh yes, that's all finished with.' Her voice sounded curiously dissatisfied.

'So what's the problem?'

'No problem. I'm blissfully happy.'

'Oh, I see. That's the problem, is it?'

'No, come on, Ag, I'm telling you, everything's fine.'

'So what did you call me up for, apart from the pleasure of hearing my voice?'

'I wanted to see how you were. Have you still got Gerry there?'

'He's still staying here, but I don't see much of him. He's working at the ice cream factory, in the cold store, making himself some money before he goes up. He may need it, if Jim doesn't come through with the parental contribution.'

'Oh.' A silence.

'Polly, why don't you tell me what's wrong?' Agatha said patiently. Polly abandoned pretence.

'Because I don't know myself. Ag, have you ever had the feeling that everything's happening sort of at arm's length?'

'With Brian?'

'Yes. I can't seem to get to grips with him. But there's nothing I can put my finger on—it's just as if he isn't really there. Or I'm not. I don't know which.'

'It was like that with Phil, always, only neither of us recognized it. I was too busy, and he, well he wasn't capable of recognizing anything so non-material. It was like listening to music with ear-muffs on.'

'Or trying to screw with a sheet between you.'

'You know why it is, don't you? He isn't right for you, Pol.'

'You always come back to that.' She sounded irritable. 'He happens to be the one I want.'

'What you want and what you get and what's good for you are hardly ever the same thing. Look what's happened before—look at Paul—'

'Oh him!'

'It'll only happen again, Polly, you know it will. As long as you keep trying to play down to them.'

'Why down? You seem to suggest I'm better than them.'

'All right, or up—it doesn't matter which. If you don't play in tune, everything will be wrong. If they're sharp of you, or flat, it will never come out right.'

'You could spend your whole life looking for someone who plays in tune with you—and never find them. Just think of the odds, Ag. I can't live alone all my life. I don't like it. And anyway, *they* do it, why shouldn't I? Thousands of people do it—'

'I know, I know. And thousands of people are unhappy. In the end, when there's nothing else left, you've got to be satisfied with yourself.'

'I sometimes think,' she said painfully, 'that these eastern religions are right. All this insistence on self is what makes us unhappy.'

'Oh yes, there's a fine sense of fulfilment to be had from abandoning yourself. Complete surrender—to God, if you're religious. To a man, if you're an old-fashioned anti-feminist.'

'Now you're being sarcastic.'

'Not really. I mean it, I can see the appeal of giving up responsibility for yourself. But that's what it is—giving up. If you can do it, fine. But some of us—and you're one—can't do it. Once you've accepted responsibility, anything else is a cop-out. And you never really give up completely, not *really*. You always hold something back. And they know it. It doesn't satisfy them either.'

'So what's the answer?' she said miserably.

'There's no answer, is there?'

'It seems—not,' Agatha said unwillingly. 'Unless you can find someone who thinks like you and is willing to have an evenly balanced partnership. But they're about as rare as hen's teeth, I think.'

Polly was silent. Agatha said sadly, 'They should never have given us education. It only made us miserable. Made us aware of all the things we could never have.'

'Oh you're just a bloody pessimist,' she said crossly. 'There must be a way, there has to be a way.'

'That's my girl. Keep on fighting. *Noli illegitimi—*'

'Oh Ag, I do love you.'

'I love you too. Go out there and give 'em hell, kid.'

* * *

Mid-afternoon, a wet, chilly afternoon, full of the sound of rain on dying leaves and intimations of mortality. Summer seemed over. She would have liked to light a fire, but it would not have been worth it, since she had a concert at seven-thirty. The doorbell rang as she was about to get into a bath to warm herself up. She cursed wearily and put on her warm dressing-gown and padded downstairs. It was Jim Blackburn, his dark hair flat to his head with rain.

'I couldn't remember what number it was. I walked up and down the street twice before I thought to look for your car.'

'You'd better come in,' she said, stepping backwards into the hall. The shadow of the porch had been upon her; as she moved into the light from the drawing-room door, he made a muted sound of surprise.

'Christ, Aggie, I wouldn't have known you. Malcolm said you'd changed, but I never thought . . .'

'Come in properly, so I can shut the door.'

'But, are you ill? Have you seen a doctor? I mean, Christ, Aggie, you look terrible.'

'Thanks.'

'No really though, I think you should see a doctor.'

'I saw one. She said there was nothing wrong with me, so I didn't go back. She said it was all my imagination, and how could I prove otherwise?'

She led him into the drawing-room, and he stood just inside the door, his hands hanging, looking helpless and troubled.

'It's nice of you to be concerned,' she said. He looked at her sharply.

'I'm not entirely heartless, you know.'

There was a silence. He seemed unable to take his eyes off her, and unable to say what it was he came for. She said,

'Would you like a drink?'

He seemed about to refuse, but then

accepted. She got them both whisky, and then to make him sit down, sat herself on the edge of the sofa, and waited for him to get to it. It had to be about Gerry—it was more years than she could remember since he had come to see her.

He had worn well, she thought, and kept his figure. Though that heart-breaking beauty he had had as a young man was gone, he was still very attractive, attractive enough to get almost any woman he wanted. She wondered what his wants were now: Diana was not the woman he would have chosen years ago, and she wondered whether his looks had not outlasted his desires. She felt strangely attached to him, as if strong delicate threads ran from him to her, along which the pulses of his life beat still. She had loved him once; he was perhaps the only man she had ever loved; but she had grown up, and he had stayed as he was, and the years stretched the threads that bound her to him so that she could see him far off and unchanged at the other end of time, as much hers as he had ever been, and simultaneously close up, a shrugged-off husk like a discarded snake-skin. His unreality made her feel more solid, and she was grateful for that, solidity being a thing she had not felt much recently.

'Is Gerry here?' he asked at last. He did not look at her, and she knew he was going to say something he thought would hurt her. He had always avoided her eyes when he was going to hurt her. She missed the old sinking feeling she had always had on those occasions; she did not want to admit that he could not hurt her any longer; she did not want him to have to know it, because he was still the Jim she had loved, and she was responsible for him.

'No, he's at work. He's got himself a job for a few weeks, until he goes up.'

'Agatha, I've come here to appeal to your better nature,' he said. It came out abrupt and harsh, and she recognized it for something he had practised in the car on the way over. 'Lord knows, by now I ought to have accepted that you haven't got a better nature, but I can't help hoping that some decency still lingers on in you. I've come to ask you to let Gerry go.'

'I can't—' she began, but he cut her off.

'We have so little time with him left—children grow up so quickly. I don't suppose any consideration of us could sway you, but I have to suppose you have some feelings for the boy, so for his sake, please, let him go. Think what it will mean to him in years to come when he looks back on this. I'm sorry for you, if you've really been ill—and God knows you look ill—but—'

'Jim, I can't let him go, because I don't have him,' she interrupted gently. He opened his mouth to speak again, but she went on, 'Jim! Listen to me before you go on. Gerry doesn't belong to me. He is staying here because he wants to, that's all. If he wants to go, he can go.'

Jim looked at her now, bitterly. 'Oh yes, you can play with words. Of course he's free to go—except that you know damn well he won't leave you as long as you keep your claws in him. Christ almighty, do you think I've forgotten? I was infatuated with you for two years—I know how hard it was to tear myself away.'

'The difference was, you and I were lovers.'

He goggled. 'You're trying to tell me you and he aren't lovers?'

'That's what I'm trying to tell you.'

'And you expect me to believe it?'

'Not really. You make up your mind about things before you ever come to them, and so you generally find what you're looking for. I know you, Jim, you haven't changed. You'll only ever see the evidence that fits with your theories—the rest you'll ignore.'

'Agatha, please let him go.' He looked into her eyes now, still not seeing her, but making an appeal on a different level which demanded the gesture. 'You loved me once, I believe that; he's all we have. He's all *I* have. Diana's left me—you didn't know that, did you? Maggie and I—well, Gerry has always been everything to us. For God's sake, Agatha—he's all I have.'

'Oh Jim, you make so much of it. Nothing's that important. Our lives are so small and short and pointless, nothing really matters. You don't have Gerry, you never did, any more than I did. He belongs to himself. You can't ever own anybody, but people like you and Maggie go on making those desperate futile efforts, and breaking everything in the process.'

'Not you,' he said bitterly. 'I never broke you.'

'No. Did you want to?'

'You're too inhuman to be broken. I can see now it was a waste of time trying to appeal to you. You're as cold as you are hard. Better feelings!' He gave a short, theatrical laugh. 'You wouldn't know what they were if you were handed them on a plate. You never did have any morals. You'd jump into bed with anyone. You jumped into bed with me quick enough—and now you're taking my son away from me. Aren't you ashamed of yourself? But no, you wouldn't know how.'

She watched him unmoved. There was nothing that was worth while answering, except in what he had not said. 'Why do you hate yourself so much, Jim? You shouldn't—it isn't worth it.'

'Hate myself? That's a good one!'

'I loved you once; you shouldn't take that away from yourself.'

He stared at her, and she saw his mouth begin to quiver, and she was across the room to him before he could break, on her knees in front of him, taking him in her arms, and there was a fraction of a second of resistance before he relaxed against her, his arms going round her neck, his face nuzzling into her.

'Darling, darling, don't,' she murmured, holding him tightly.

'Oh Agatha, help me,' he cried, muffled by her body. 'Diana's left me. I've got nothing, nothing at all. My life is so empty. If I lose Gerry too—'

There was nothing she could say that he would listen to, nothing he would understand, nothing she could do to help him. She let him tell her about Diana, too young and strong for him, hard and beautiful and confident, tiring of his middle-aged softness, his growing dependence on her. She had not been willing to give what he asked, and goaded by the increasing restraint he placed on her, had turned and rended him at last, made cruel by desperation. He was a middle-aged, mediocre trumpet-player with a failed marriage and the end of his career in sight, and all he had had was his reputation, his sexual prowess, to bolster him up; and his beautiful young mistress had smashed that at a stroke.

Agatha stroked his head, racked with pity for the frailty of his life, the tenuous hold he had had upon the world. She had been young when he had shattered her illusions, forced her to face up to reality, forced her to take up the responsibility for her own life which never again could she lay down. In a sense he had destroyed her chances of happiness, crippled her ability to live the normal semi-conscious life that most people lived; but he came to her now, and the very desperation that had sent him to her, of all people, moved her.

His clinging turned to an embrace, he began to grope at her, needing to prove somewhere, on someone, that he was still himself, and she let him. She took him up to bed, let him screw her, even responded, made him think he could still excite and satisfy her; because it was all she could give him, and it cost her nothing. It didn't matter. Nothing mattered any more, not for her, not like this; because it was September the twenty-ninth, and she had missed the fourth period in a row since Bristol, and she knew against all reason and all possibility that she was pregnant.

CHAPTER TWELVE

Gerry, packing.

'You're looking very pale about the ears. Like a skinned rabbit.'

'I expect that's my haircut. When I said I wanted it short his eyes lit up. You'd think he was on piece-work.'

He was making a valiant effort. 'I will drive you up if you want. It's a longish walk from the station to your college, you know.'

'I could take a taxi. Or a bus.'

'I hadn't though of that.' Silence while he fished in the back of a drawer and came out with a crumpled piece of lining-paper.

'I think that's all.'

'If there's anything else I can send it on.'

'Or keep it for me.'

'Yes. I wish you would contact your father.'

'No.'

'He's very unhappy. Your mother too, I expect.'

'It's his own fault.'

'That's a very condemnatory attitude. Our miseries are mostly our own faults. He wants to see you.'

'I'm not responsible for him.'

They went downstairs. It was dark outside, the air cool and smelling of smoke. Autumn advancing in scarlet battalions. The orchards would be almost bare now, the apples all wrapped and stored, and only the great ilex tree on the south side of the house still clad. She shook her head to clear it. Gerry was staring at her.

'Agatha, please let me visit. It isn't far from Oxford. I could come at weekends.'

'No. No visits.'

'Please.'

'It's time you lived your own life.'

'I love you.'

'You're not responsible for me.'

It was said to make him smile, but her dark eyes were remote, and he could see she was withdrawing.

'Agatha.' He took her hand. 'You mustn't give up. You must keep on fighting.'

She did not answer, not even by the lift of an eyebrow. She was quite still, only waiting for him to go. His shoulders went down.

'You'll let me write? And you'll write back?'

'Oh yes, we can exchange letters.'

He had to be content with that. He picked up his case. 'Let me come and see you at Christmas.' A long silence. He was about to repeat the question when she said quietly, as if absently, 'We'll see.' He kissed her turned cheek, and it felt cold, almost rubbery, as he imagined the flesh of a corpse would feel. 'Goodbye.'

At the gate he turned to look back, and she was just going into the house. It seemed to close round her with finality and he felt helpless and lost. He was so afraid he would never see her again.

* * *

She went up to bed, climbing slowly and steadily like one who has a long journey, carrying her body like a wound, carefully, lest movement should jolt a dull pain into sharpness. She had let Gerry go, flung him up into the sky like a pigeon, and the air was full of the clatter of wings, but she could not yet feel free of him, not while his thoughts kept homing on her. Other people tied us to life more firmly than our own concerns. He had said 'I am not responsible for them' but it was a statement of desire rather than conviction. Freedom from responsibility could only be given, never taken, and he would bear their need like a tax as long as they levied it.

To her bedroom, the door always open, and through the door

she saw the room dimly lit sun never came round this side of the house narrow long room tall and papered up to the picture-rail creamy paper with red and blue lozenges and two pictures dim and brown hanging from their long triangles of cord *Raleigh's Boyhood* and *The Toast* in matching frames

and across to the window to draw the curtains. The fabric felt delicate under her fingers, brittle with dust. About time they were washed but it was such a job getting them down, and in any case there was no one but her to care about them. She jerked them smartly across. They were rough fawn peasant-weave

they were creamy with rust-coloured trees all over them

from Marks and Spencers. She was tired, tired, her eyes heavy and cold in their sockets like oysters, stationary and numb. She turned from the window

to the dim room the two beds narrow virginal couches or one was where Nellie slept on the side by the gas fire her own opposite brown lino on the floor and a rag rug by each bedside home-made by Mrs Holloway and in the hearth a battered tin saucepan in which Nellie heated milk for them before they went to bed Nellie was worried about her but how could she tell her about

and crossed to her bed, shrugging off the robe and letting it drop on the floor. She climbed in between the sheets and lay down on her back. She was tired, but she wouldn't sleep. Sleep came when it would, and between whiles her brain revolved goaded and heavy like a dying bull stuck all with coloured lances. How could she, how could anyone ever, how could she anymore tell the difference between reality and imagination? What had happened to her was impossible, but it had happened. Or she thought it had happened, and once she had wondered if she had imagined it all, reality shredded round her, curled up on itself like nylon touched by a flame. It was worse in daylight, because then there seemed to be some rules that she was violating; it was worse when there was someone there. Alone, and in the dark, everything was unreal, and there was no more dichotomy. She was glad Gerry was gone

(if he was gone if he had ever been there)

and she was alone. It was a long time since he had been able to ease the loneliness she felt backed up against the wall and battling. He was still all around her, but that would pass;

gradually the pigeons settled and the air grew still and she waited

in the dark scented with apples
for him to come.

*　　　*　　　*

Daylight, and from somewhere hauling up the will-power to get up and go to work. That's all it was, will; nothing inside, an empty brittle shell and yet the sense of her own courage gave her courage. She sat beside Malcolm and in front of her music-stand, beside Bill and beyond him Mike, and all around her the accustomed shape and sound of the orchestra; her home and family. Malc was telling her about a car he had seen, a 1956 Dodge, and how he had tailed it half across London in order to be able to ask the driver where he had got it and if he would sell it. On the other side Bill was telling Mike a story, one of his anecdotes held together with fuckin's as a ship's plates were held with rivets. A riveting story. Mike was listening with his face already composed for laughter; now and then his eye caught Agatha's with amused complicity; good-old-Bill was written on his face. Her family. She was good-old-Aggie, old Aggo, or even Aggro, one of the boys, accepted slowly and hesitantly, but in the end completely. Aggo was all right. You could say what you liked to her. And she was good. That was important.

Professional.

Home and family, all she had ever had. Chronically sociable, congenitally an outsider, always wanting a gang to belong to. Orphanage kid, never had pals at school, never really had a home, no family, but they let her belong to their gang, and for that she would have been anything they wanted her to. All things to all men, so flexible, the boneless wonder, that in the end it was impossible to tell what her character really was. Perhaps she didn't have one.

'Gentlemen, trumpets, can we have those staccatos really short, really crisp—tak-tak-tak-tak ta.' The conductor pricked them in the air with his finger. Malc gave him a responsible look and a grave nod. He was their leader, he would see to it, yessir. Sarnt Malc, interpreting the officer's demands, and conveying with them his own contempt, his robust down-to-earthness, officers were effete but sergeants were all right, okay lads, give the old bastard what he wants. They played. They weren't really making much of an effort yet. All of them except Bill were playing one-handed, throwing out the notes idly, knowing the moment for proof was not yet, exuding professional competence from the back row so that the conductor would know when the time came it would be all right. The section took its character from its leader. When Agatha had first played with them the leader had been a man of obvious virtue and paraded integrity, and then they had played everything, all the run-throughs, as if they were the real thing. The section, but particularly the second, took the leader's character. A good second had to be flexible. A chameleon.

'I hear poor old Jimbo's having a hard time,' Malc said. He swung his hooter idly between his knees, but his eye was sharp and observant out of the corner.

'What's happened?' she asked.

'Well, you know his bird threw him over and he went back to his missus?'

'Yeah. Well, he never did have any taste. I mean, you only had to look at her to know it wouldn't last.'

'Hard bitch.'

'That's what I thought.'

'Not her, you. Anyway, apparently Maggie tried to do herself in.'

They played a couple of bars.

'Why?'

'Dunno. Something to do with the kid, I think. Have you—'

'No, I haven't still got him, if that's what you were going to ask.'

They played.

'He's gone to university. How is Maggie?'

'Well, she didn't make a proper job of it, but she's a bit of a cotcase. But I wouldn't be surprised if it wasn't the making of Jimbo in the end, you know. He's the sort of bloke 'at needs someone to look after. I never really thought all this big talk was really him, you know, cocksmanship and chasing the birds. Underneath it all—'

'He was a real pipe-and-slippers man, eh?'

Malcolm eyed her with interest. 'You knew him pretty well once, didn't you? What did you think?'

'I was too young then to know much about him. I was more interested in my own life. When you're young you don't tend to see the whole of a person, only those bits that relate to you.'

Malcolm jeered automatically. 'Thank you and good night.' But he reached out a hand all the same and squeezed her knee. 'According to what I heard, he treated you like shit.'

'Pretty well everything we do to each other seems to turn out like that, doesn't it?' She returned the squeeze. 'Except you and me, Malc. We're just good friends.'

'I wouldn't be too sure of that, kid,' he said, and his bootsole eye rested flat on her face for a moment before the conductor called,

'Right, gentlemen, the scherzo please,' and they turned their pages and concentrated.

Jim Blackburn, so much a part of history. He had got to the philosophical state where his name achieved meaning as well as reference. She had been twenty when she met him, very young for her age, just up at the Royal College; Jim was ten years older, excitable, restless, dissatisfied, wondering what direction his life was going to take. He was principal in one of the London Big Four then—that was before Maggie persuaded him to go freelance in the hope that she would see more of him. In the event it only meant it was harder for her to keep track of where he should be, but then nothing would have improved the situation. That was another of the fallacies of youth, that people could be changed, that relationships could be directed and improved, like intensive farming. But Jim had a basic need to be unfaithful, uncontrollable, untraceable, unpredictable, and it was not a feature of his relationship with Maggie. He needed her to deceive. If he had by accident married a woman who didn't care if he screwed around with other women, he would have divorced her and found one who did. It was Maggie's misfortune that she really cared, and cared about caring.

But how can you know that at the time? Agatha fell in love with him, with his glossy good looks, his devil-may-careity, with screwing him. She knew little of sex and thought that it was good because it was with him, that the excitement was a function of him. But when the first butterfly-dust of illusion wore off, she found that she loved him too, absurdly, illogically, everything about him, from the way he scratched his head during pauses to the way his left knee turned a little out when he walked. The whole fabric of him was precious.

She didn't know about Maggie, not for a long time. They had a wonderful affair, and it never occurred to her to think it strange that they always met at her lodgings or in public, that they never went to his house. Then one day she met Maggie at a concert. She knew her vaguely by sight—she was a singer of modest reputation. Agatha had just spent four days at the Edinburgh Festival with Jim. Maggie, who was talking to Agatha through geographical accident, was saying,

'My husband wanted me to come with him to Edinburgh, but my mother hasn't been well and I really didn't think I ought to leave her. He was terribly disappointed. He simply hates these provincial tours, he can't bear doing them alone.'

'Which one is your husband?' Agatha asked, but the fraction of a second before the answer came she knew it already.

'Jim Blackburn. He plays trumpet—do you know him?'

'Not very well,' Agatha had said; and remembered that Jim had asked her at the last moment, and had said, 'Please come—I hate touring by myself.'

What she had minded most of all was being made to feel guilty when she had done nothing wrong. Jim, in his inimitable fashion, had refused to apologize or even allow that what he did was dastardly. That was one of his charms, his complete assumption of amorality. They had gone on being lovers until she had got pregnant, and then he had backed off in alarm, dropped her like a hot potato and somehow or other never managed to get to see her. She had fallen heavily down the platform stairs in Earl's Court tube station and lost the baby, and after that he had come back to her, but it wasn't the same, and lasted only a few weeks more before habit and custom and comfort had driven him back into the fold, leaving Agatha to start building up the wall again.

And she had never managed to blame him; and she had never managed after that to love anyone with that same absoluteness. The damaged knee is never wholly sound again. Lacking a dimension she had gone on, building herself a life. There had been two more men; serious relationships that is, rather than casual affairs; Simon, whom she had lived with for nearly three years, and Phil whom she had married, and both had broken down in the end. Both had gone off after other relationships, and Agatha had spent months and months after each trying to convince herself she cared, and doing a good job on the whole. Only now, with hindsight, with the ability to compare with other people's experiences, she could see that it was all pointless, that none of it mattered, that she didn't care at all, really. Unsound, favouring a limb, she had not really been in the race.

Only work was real, being here, one of the boys, with her family, making music, perched on the surface of this wildly spinning world like a fly on a humming-top; she could look down at herself from sufficient height to get a good perspective, and see that the thing she had lost which Jim and Gerry and Maggie and Polly and Malc and the others still had was the ability to deceive herself.

The rehearsal broke and the orchestra fragmented. Agatha shook the spit out of her trumpet, and began packing away. She was aware Malcolm was fidgeting, but took no heed until Bill said,

'Are you coming for a drink, Malc?'

'No thanks, Bill, I want to talk to Aggie.'

'Oh well, don't do anyone I wouldn't do.'

Then Aggie looked up and saw Malc's expression. She straightened up slowly. Malcolm fished in his inside pocket and drew out a long envelope and held it out to her.

'I volunteered to give you this, Ag,' he said. 'I think you can guess what it is.'

'You tell me,' she suggested. He looked angry.

'Come on, you know. You want me to say it? We're giving you the push. You're out, fired, sacked, finito. Okay?'

'You don't need to be angry,' she said. 'Why should you feel guilty?'

'I'm not guilty,' he said, whipping up his

flames in protection. 'You know it had to happen. I mean, Christ, look at you. Do you know what you look like? Do you remember what you used to be like?'

'Oh yes,' she said, 'I do.' She had a vivid picture in her mind of herself as she used to be, happy, laughing, vivacious, sparkling blue eyes and long dark ringlets blowing in the salty marsh wind. No, that was someone else—

'I'm sorry, Ag, but it couldn't go on, you know that. We had a meeting on Monday, and we voted on it, and I said I wanted to tell you myself. It was only right. After all—'

'You are my sergeant,' she said. 'We've played well together, haven't we? I was the best second you ever had.'

'You *were*.' He placed the emphasis firmly. 'Aggie,' he said more gently, 'why don't you see a specialist? There might be something they can do for you.'

'There's nothing anyone can do any more, Malc.'

She hadn't quite meant him to take it like that, but she saw the fear and distress yawn in his face; and behind it, barely discernible, a kind of relief that someone else was going through the door instead of him, as if there were an annual quota that he would not now be called upon to fill.

'Oh Christ, Ag, I never thought—'

'Don't think. Listen, pal, shall we go and have a drink? C'mon, one last time?'

‘Okay. I’ll have to phone home—Mary’s expecting me. But it’ll only take a moment. I’ll meet you by the lift.’

She smiled to herself as he hurried off. He would want to be out of earshot of her while he explained to his wife. Principal Cornet Player’s Mid-day Mercy Dash—Wife Consents, she headlined to herself. Once we joked all the time, and I was one of the lads, and now I am filled with death. It is impossible that I am pregnant, therefore what I am carrying must be a tumour, and I will die of it, because I will not seek help. I am dying of the inability to distinguish between reality and imagination; or perhaps of the inability to care which is which.

She finished packing up, shrugged on her blazer, and sauntered off the platform and towards the exit, and she felt strangely light, as if one of her responsibilities had been shouldered by someone else.

CHAPTER THIRTEEN

Withdrawing into winter. Now that Gerry was gone and she had no work, and Polly was too busy with her own life to call, she found herself withdrawing, like an animal hibernating, holing up for the long winter. She stayed in bed late, sometimes sleeping in the mornings as soon as it got light and drowsing through to lunchtime or later. Often she did not bother to dress, but wandered about in her dressing-gown. In any case, her clothes fitted her so badly it was a trial to put them on. They were all too long, but on the other hand, now she had started to swell up, some of them were also too tight. She would spend a long time in front of the mirror, studying the body she saw. Smaller than her own, shorter and slighter, fair-haired, but with those flat dark eyes that looked out from a depth of time that seemed to go back into eternity; from under the small breasts the belly surged forward, stretching the navel open and flat: from a winkle-shell to a dimple.

He had left her alone for a long time; now with the full moon he came back, standing at the foot of her bed in the dry, sleepless, blue-white moonlit bedroom, smiling at her. He liked to tease her a little, he liked her to want him to come to her, and he would stand there just looking and smiling until her body began to tingle for him, until she began to long for the touch of his hands on her breasts. His hands were no longer cold now; still silky, sensitive; hands and mouth he would reach for her breasts, bigger now, swelling up, the blue veins showing in the white.

'That's how I like to see them,' he said. He would suckle until she writhed with wanting, and then he would reach down a gentle hand and touch her, oh so sweetly and watch her face for her pleasure. She saw his face so clearly now, a pale, fair face, small sharp features and those huge, ruined eyes, blue weary sad eyes, old-young, netted with fine wrinkles, eyes of pain and memory, eyes that had seen all and survived, eyes for whom humour love joy pleasure peace were conscious achievements. She wanted him, she was lonely and she wanted him, and when he came into her she felt completed, like a puzzle with the last piece put into place. He never hurt her, he was very gentle and careful, holding himself clear of her with his arms and pushing slowly and carefully until excitement overcame them and they thrust at each other with abandon. Abandon. That was what she wanted now, but it never quite, quite came, and she would see the sadness in his eyes in the moment before his dispersed, dislimned; the image of the sad, ancient eyes would remain and the air would be full of the breath of words, love me love me love me.

She saw the rooms, sometimes one on top of the other, superimposed so delicately that it was hard to tell which was which and it made her dizzy to reach for something not knowing which reality it existed in, an ornament from one room resting on the table from another. The room with the dark brown-sprigged paper and the brass bedstead, the attic room, the room with the pictures, the bare white room with the crucifix on the wall, her own bedroom with the peasant-weave curtains, the apple-loft, others less easy to distinguish. She knew he brought them in with him, as a man coming in from out of doors will bring the smell of grass and earth and rain with him. She knew he was there sometimes when she could not see him. She saw him best when there was moonlight, for he was made of shadows and they were rich and black and strong when there was moonlight. When he lay on her now, she could not see herself through him; and as he grew more, she grew less. Light passed through her, she would sometimes see shadows of things behind her through her own reflection in the mirror, things that were there and things that were not there.

She spoke to him through the glass at first, but then perceiving she did not need the glass, she spoke to him in her mind, then aloud, hearing his answers though they had no sound. Who am I? she would ask, and he would tell her Agatha. That seemed the only reality, and yet the name had reference but no meaning. There was nothing she could attach to the sounds of Agatha; her sense of her own identity was eroded away.

The firelight brought him too, if she turned off the lights. The flames would jump in the chimney, and the shadows would lick up the walls, surging in the corners and gathering behind furniture, and she would glimpse him, half-see him. If she kept still and quiet, he would come to her, stand behind her and stroke her hair, and she would smell the salt-marsh air, or the damp sweetness of earth and grass, or the ripe golden smell of apples.

The room then fogged and flowed into itself, drawing its other realities out of itself as a conjurer draws coloured silks out of a hat. Then she began at last to understand.

This has all happened before, hasn't it, she asked, and he consented. These were the constants, the boy, and the smell of apples, and the falling in the darkness: the man cut out dark against the light in the doorway. I am Agatha, and you are—but there it ended. She did not know him, though she recognized him. He came from the same deep places as the dark eyes of the woman whose reflection she saw when she looked into the mirror. But if that were she, what had happened to the Agatha she had been? What had happened to the tall dark bright-eyed girl that had been Agatha? Or was she still there, superimposed like all the rooms one on the other? But no, there was no sense of that when she looked in the mirror. There were many rooms but only one she. Agatha was gone, or had never existed.

There were days and days, she could hardly call them better or worse, because she had no standpoint to view them from. But there were days when she went down to the Guildhall to teach, and streets and traffic and red buses and office workers seemed the normality and she felt obscurely happy, as if something had been proved. There were days when she went out shopping, and felt a sense of achievement from buying bread and toilet rolls and oranges and cheese. And there were days when the rooms flowed so chaotically around her that she hardly dared to move, feeling her way forward inch by inch like someone lost in a pea-souper, afraid of falling down the stairs or the loft ladder or out of a window that painted itself under her feet on a floor which was a ceiling; days when finding a window by feel she would look out and sway dizzily at the multiplicity of views and perspectives massing themselves beyond the glass like wolves beyond the circle of dying firelight.

And then Polly rang her. The sound sharpened the edges of things and she picked up the telephone without hesitation.

'Ag, it's me. Are you all right?'

'Yes, but you aren't. What's happened?'

'Can I come round? Are you in?'

'Yes, come. I'll leave the door on the latch. Just come in.'

'Why, what's wrong? Are you in bed?'

'I'm not sure. But come round anyway.'

But it was a day when things stayed still. The door was where she thought she remembered it had always been, and when Polly arrived a quarter of an hour later Agatha was sitting in, to the best of her knowledge, an armchair in the drawing room. Polly came in, calling, and stopped on the threshold of the drawing room staring in pity and horror before she came over and knelt on the floor in front of Agatha.

'Oh God,' was all she could say for a while. 'Oh God.'

'I've changed?' Agatha suggested after a moment. She put her arms round Polly, and Polly flinched for a second before she returned the embrace.

'Oh Agatha, it's terrible. I can't bear it. What have you done to deserve this?'

'It's all right, it doesn't hurt,' she said gently.

'Oh Agatha, don't joke.' She pulled her head back and searched the face and form in front of her for some vestige of the person she had known. There was only the faintest of resemblances, as between a parent and a child who really resembles the other parent, just a hint of likeness in the face as a whole, which could not be pinned down. 'You've changed out of all recognition,' Polly said quietly. 'It must be terrible for you. How can you bear it?'

Agatha looked carefully at Polly, saw the dark shadows under the eyes and the tell-tale puffiness of the eyelids. 'You're in trouble too. What is it?'

'I came here to cry on your shoulder,' Polly admitted, 'but it seems so trivial compared with what's happened to you. Is there anything they can do for you? I mean, can it be reversed or halted? Do they know what it is?'

'They? There is no they.'

'You haven't had any medical treatment?'

'For what? Who would believe me?'

'But if I told them—if you showed them photographs—'

'They would not believe they were photographs of me. Would you? And they would not believe you. Things that can't be measured, and that don't match up with any known pattern, can't be believed. Rejecting the impossible is what keeps us sane.'

'But—'

'Don't. Tell me what's wrong. I don't want to talk about me. There's nothing wrong with me.'

'Nothing—?'

'Except that I am not myself. That's a joke,' she added gently. 'What's happened?'

Polly's focus changed from Agatha's face to her own inward scenery, and a bitterness touched her mouth and her eyes filled with tears. 'Can't you guess?'

'Brian?'

Nod.

'And Janice?'

'Oh no. That was all over. I know you never believed he was going to give her up, but he did. No, it's somebody else now, this girl at the office where he works, Geraldine. He'd been having drinks with her after work and I thought nothing of it—after all, I wasn't going to put him on a collar and lead and tell him he mustn't speak to anyone but me ever again. And now it turns out that she—that he's been screwing her, and he says it's getting serious. He says she wants to move in with him.'

'*She* wants to move in with *him*?'

'That's the way he put it. As if it's nothing to do with him. He says she needs him, and he's very fond of her. I said *I* need you, and he said oh no, you're strong, you don't need anyone, least of all me.'

She swallowed and blinked, and with an effort dragged up the final fragment of shrapnel. 'And the terrible thing is, in a way he's right. And yet I don't want to be alone, I don't want to lose him, I don't want to be strong. I want him. I can't bear it. If he's right it means I'll never have anyone, that they'll always do the same thing to me, and then one day I won't be strong enough, and I'll break up. Why do they do it to us, Ag? Why do we have to want them?'

'I don't know.'

'It's going to go on being like that, isn't it? He'll take everything, and give nothing, and I'll put up with it, always hoping he means more than he says and that this time it will be different, until in the end he meets someone else, not better, just newer, and when I cry he'll say I always said I didn't want to get involved. I knew you'd get hurt. As if it wasn't anything he could have prevented, me getting hurt.'

No sound in the room but the soft hiss and

crack of the fire.

'And the trouble is, I can't even hate her, because she's just like me really, and he's going to do the same thing to her, and she'll cry when he leaves her, and he'll say he was always afraid she would get hurt. I can't bear it any more.'

She cried, not noisily, but painfully. Agatha held her, not saying anything because there was no comfort she could give. She thought of Jim and his need to shock and deceive. Brian needed to hurt for much the same reason, to prove his identity, just as Polly needed to have a love affair to prove hers. How do we know it's us without that constant proof, measuring up against the yardstick we choose for ourselves with such an unreasonable instinct for self-torture? Love me, Polly cried, because I don't know who I am otherwise; others cried suffer for me when I leave you, be angry with me when I deceive you, obey when I command you, cringe when I inflict pain and humiliation on you: that's who I am. There's nothing to be afraid of, and I am afraid of it. I am so afraid that when I look in the mirror, there will be no reflection, there will be nothing there at all.

Polly quietened, and she said, her voice low and desperate, 'I can't go through it all again. I can't. I can't face it.'

'You have to.'

'It isn't worth it. For what? No one loves me. I am nothing to anyone.'

'I love you,' Agatha said. Polly looked up, and her anger drained away, leaving her with a desolation she had professed but had not felt; she saw the emptiness in Agatha's eyes, and saw that there really was no hope, that things would not be made better because she had cried out that they were bad. If wishes were horses, someone would export them live for pet food; but though life was hopeless, it was all there was. There were depths she had not plumbed, and probably never would, and life was going to be bad enough even without them.

'I love you too,' she said slowly. 'But it isn't the same thing.'

The chaos and oblivion had always been there; self-deception was the only defence.

* * *

Forewarned by Polly's letter, but not forearmed. A small, fair woman he had never seen before opened the door. Dishevelled yellow hair like wheat straw, a drained, white face and staring dark eyes, thin hands clutching a too-big dressing-gown around her body. He tried to speak, but his mouth was dry. She looked up at him, and recognition faded in, and she smiled, and only then did he know her.

'Hello Gerry. What are you doing here?'

'I came to see you. You didn't answer my

letters.'

'Didn't I? Shouldn't you be at college?'

'We've come down for the Christmas vac. Agatha, are you all right? I've been so worried about you.' She didn't answer him, but glanced back over her shoulder into the house as if checking that something or someone was not visible. 'Have you got someone here?'

'Do you want to come in?' she said. 'I'm sorry I'm not dressed. I don't bother usually, unless I'm going out.' She looked over her shoulder again, and then moved back to allow him in. He waited while she closed the door behind him and then took her by the shoulders. He would have drawn her to him and held her, but something in her face forbade it.

'Are you all right?'

'Yes, why not?'

'You don't look all right. I think you need help. I think you should be in a hospital. Won't you let me get you a doctor, or take you to hospital?'

'I'm all right, Gerry. And shouldn't you be at home? Have you spoken to your parents?'

He was distracted as she meant him to be. 'I'm going to them afterwards. Dad came and visited me in Oxford, and we sorted it all out. You know Mum was ill?'

'I heard something about it.'

'Well they've patched it all up because of that, and I've promised to spend Christmas with them. But I had to come and see you first. Why didn't you answer my letters?'

'Oh, I've had a lot on my mind. Anyway, I didn't want to encourage you.'

'Encourage me?'

'To waste your time. You've got your own life to lead.'

'You're part of my life.'

'No, I'm not.'

'You must allow me to be the judge of that. It is my life, after all.'

'I can't cope with you, Gerry. You're a strain on me. I haven't the energy.'

He would not be offended. 'Are you still having the dream?'

'It doesn't trouble me any more.' She had forgotten he had heard that before.

'That's what your mother said. So you are still having it?'

'It's only a dream, and as I said, it doesn't worry me now.'

She tried to go past him into the house, and he stopped her, and in the narrow hallway her body brushed against him. His eyes widened in shock. For a long time he stared into her eyes, trying to read facts. Then at last he said,

'How long?' She didn't answer and he shook her by the shoulders, not roughly, but hard. 'How long have you been pregnant?'

'Five months,' she said at last, without emphasis. He goggled, and she saw him trying to work it back.

'Was it that bloke you were with when I first came here?'

'That was June,' she said. 'Don't you remember it was midsummer eve when you came and chased him away?'

'Oh.' He let her go and turned away, hurt, and when he spoke again she could tell that he was trying not to cry. 'So you were having an affair with someone all the time I was here. Who was it?' He turned back, his eyes bright with anger. 'Was it that precious Malcolm of yours? I always thought you were very good friends.'

'No, it wasn't Malcolm.' She spoke patiently against his sarcasm. His eyes widened.

'Oh God, it wasn't my father, was it?'

'The only person I slept with here was you,' she said. She saw his face struggling hand to hand with his brain.

'But we didn't—I mean I never—I never made love to you.' There was the faintest hint of a question, as if he supposed he might have done it in his sleep and missed it. She took him by the hand, reassuringly, and led him into the drawing-room. A bottle of scotch and a jug of water were on the side table, and she said,

'Have a drink. You look as if you need it. Make me one too. Lots of water and just a little scotch to disinfect it. Water's not to be drunk neat you know—fish fuck in it.'

The therapy did him good, and by the time he had prepared two drinks and brought her one he was able to sit calmly on the sofa and speak in a normal tone. Only his eyes kept getting away from him to stare at her belly and had to be hauled back to her face.

'Please tell me, Agatha. Don't play games with me. Whose baby is it?'

She sighed and looked away towards the window. 'It isn't anyone's, chuck. I didn't screw with anyone. It's just a baby. It's there, that's all I know.'

'But—but that just isn't possible.'

'Isn't it? I wonder. People have claimed it before, but naturally enough no one ever gives them credit for telling the truth. Spontaneous cell-division? Why not? I can conceive of it.'

'Agatha, are you sure—I mean—'

'Am I sure its mine?'

'Don't joke, please. Are you sure it's a baby?'

'I thought of that a long time ago, and for a long time that's what I told myself. But now it moves.' He winced, averting his face. 'It's a baby all right.'

'Then couldn't you have an abortion?'

'No.'

'But surely—'

'No.' She outstared his protest silently. It was too late now. Her mind still rejected what her body postulated, and the only resolution of the dichotomy was that whatever happened to her was through Him. He was all she had, and she could not do that to Him, whether it was life or death she carried.

She waited for him to catch up with it. Finally he said, slowly and unwillingly, 'Agatha, I know it sounds crazy, but could it be something to do with—with the ghost?' She didn't answer and he went on, 'I mean, it would be impossible if it was a ghost, but could it have been a real person and you thought it was a ghost because you thought you were asleep? Oh I don't know—I just can't think it out.'

'It happened one time when you were in the bed with me,' she said. 'Do you think you wouldn't have woken if it was a real person, even if they had a key and didn't have to break in?'

He was a brave person, and she saw him brace himself for the logical follow-through. 'Then it has to be something to do with the ghost. It can't be chance. Your mother was haunted in the same way. But why? We must find out—the answer is there somewhere, if only we can find it.'

The answer? To what? What was the question? He spoke as if this were a problem that could be resolved. But she was pregnant—what could change that?

'There's nothing to be done, Gerry.'

'Yes there is—there are still lots of things we haven't tried.'

'I don't want to. I am too tired. I haven't the will, even if it would do any good.'

'Then let me!' He leaned forward eagerly, and she knew as surely as if she could read his mind that he needed the activity, he needed to feel he was doing something because he was young and had not yet learned to sit still under adversity. Action must help; he must do something positive. 'There's the photograph—we still haven't explained that. It must be something to do with your mother. So that old woman didn't recognize it, but so what? She didn't know everything. And she didn't know your mother right from the beginning. Let me try and find out about her early life.'

'How would you propose doing that?' she asked wearily. His very energy seemed to make her more brittle.

'I could go to the children's home where she was brought up, and work back from there. Find out who was there and try to speak to them. Some people in the village might remember her. Give me the photograph, and I'll show it to people and find someone who recognizes it. *Someone* must know something.'

'If it makes you feel better, then do it. How could I stop you anyway? You must do what you think fit.'

'Give me the photograph then. And you'd better give me a letter of introduction, in case anyone thinks I haven't the right to ask questions. Write a letter saying you authorize me to enquire on your behalf.'

She did what he asked, and she let him go

round to the shops and buy some eggs and cheese and cook her an omelette, and she ate it while he watched her approvingly. It was not for her, but for him, for his need to feel useful, for his need to feel he was imposing order on chaos. She was chaos, and she had frightened him badly. Already he had forgotten the impossible nature of what had happened and substituted the need for positive action. He was all right. He left her buoyantly, promising her results, admonishing her to take care of herself.

She saw him off from the door, and when he was out of sight she closed it again and turned back into the house where He was waiting for her. He had gone away when Gerry came in, and she had felt uneasy. She needed Him to be there, she was lonely and lost when He was not with her. She was not complete without Him. He smiled at her from the dark corner where the hallway turned the foot of the stairs, and she looked at him thoughtfully.

'This has all happened before, hasn't it? Did they believe my mother? But of course not. They never do. Nellie didn't. Bill didn't. When she told Bill he called her a slut and when she told Nellie her mouth went all twisted and prim and she turned away from me and left me. She hated me then—but Nellie was always jealous. And then there was—'

She stopped, catching her breath as the baby moved inside her, kicking at her belly. She placed her hands over the swollen hump, and felt the shape of a foot impress itself briefly in her flesh.

She was pregnant.

Which was impossible.

She began to scream again.

CHAPTER FOURTEEN

Marsh House was a children's home no more, but a private school, and could not help him. But Southwold is a small place, and patient enquiry gradually passed him along a line of hints and recommendations until he found himself in the fishermen's hall sitting across a wooden table from a gaunt old man with watery blue eyes and tufts of white whiskers sprouting from inappropriate places. He wore a guernsey and a fisherman's cap above, and corduroys and wellingtons below, a mixture of sailor and gardener, sea and earth, that did not seem inappropriate to an inhabitant of this place, where the marsh edged into the sea until you could not tell where one began and the other ended.

Jim Swainson was his name. He sat very still and upright, his hands resting on the table before him to either side of a pint of bitter. They were so gnarled, the joints so lumpy, that they barely looked like hands at all; pink-white, chalky skinned, as if the fingers between the joints had been eroded like the ribs of cliffs.

Gerry explained his mission slowly and patiently, and with many repeats, and offered his letter of introduction. Mr Swainson took it and looked at it, but didn't read it. He said,

'You want to know about Annie Shaw, that was sent to Marsh House as a baby, is that it?'

'That's right, Mr Swainson. Can you remember anything about her?'

'I can remember everything. I'm seventy-eight years old, but my memory's as good as ever it was,' he said with emphasis.

'I'm very glad,' Gerry said cautiously.

'But Annie Shaw I never knew much about, no. Except the manner of her being born, as you might say. But her mother, now, her I can tell you about. But that'd be no manner of use to you, eh?'

'Anything you can tell me, would be very helpful. Anything at all.'

The old man took a careful draught of beer, set down the glass again, and wiped his mouth on his hand. Gerry thought he was considering whether or not to tell what he knew, but when he spoke it seemed he had only been marshalling his thoughts, for he began abruptly,

'I were gardener's boy up the big house. Before the war, that was.'

'At Marsh House?'

'Nah! Marsh House were orphan asylum. I'm talking about the Red House, Squire's house. I went there soon as I left school, 1912 that were. Gardener's boy. Good place, as places went. My father were a fisherman, but my ma didn't want me to go to sea. I was her pet, see, being the youngest, and she wanted me home. So I went to the big house.'

Gerry waited patiently. Another draught of ale. The old eyes were inward-looking towards that calcified and familiar landscape of long-studied memories.

'Aggie Shaw was house-parlourmaid there. Bright as a button she was, boy, and as pretty as a picture, yeller hair and big brown eyes. Course, she was a lot older than me—she'd've been about twenty or twenty-two then I reckon, and I was just a kid, but I knew a pretty face when I saw one then, just as I do now, and she was—rare. She'd a nice way with her, too. Always singing about her work, and a good word to say for everyone, and never out of temper. Cook didn't like her, but then cook didn't like anyone. Thought she was too free with the gentry, and maybe she was, the way it turned out.'

The next pause was a long one, and Gerry was induced in the end to prompt him.

'Something happened to her?'

'Same as I'm telling you,' Swainson said, faintly irritable at the interruption. 'There was a friend of the young master's used to come and stay regular, come for the shooting, a real bold one, Londoner, with an eye for the girls, but no real harm in him, I never thought. Still, this Aggie caught his eye, and it wasn't long 'for she started to foller him about with her eyes, you know the way they does, like a heifer on heat. Mind you, it was a strict house, and there was no hanky-panky, but they took to meeting on the quiet, just to talk and hold hands. I used to take messages for 'em, see, that's how I knew, and I'd keep look out while they was talking, behind the potting shed or down the wild end of the orchard. But she was a good girl, was Aggie, whatever people said afterwards, and she wouldn't have nothing to do with no larking about, and he wanted her so bad he wanted to marry her, but he couldn't, acourse, her being a servant and him being his father's son.'

'Was his father a wealthy man?'

'Middling,' Mr Swainson admitted. 'But a good family. Well so things went on, and not much change about 'em, until one day Captain Hammond comes to me—'

'Who's that?'

'This young man, same as I'm telling you. He were in the Guards, same as the young master. He comes to me and he says, Jim, he says, will you take a message to her for me? And I says yessir, and he says, will you tell her to come to me in the barn after dinner tonight, cause I got something to tell her. Well I takes the message, but I thinks a bit about it, because one way and another barns is barns and dark is dark, so I keeps nearby and watches, and after he comes away I goes in to see if she's all right. And there she is, sitting in the apple loft, crying her eyes out.'

Gerry made sympathetic noises. 'Had he—?'

'Crying like her heart was broke, she was, and I says what's up, and she says, the Captain's going away and he says war's coming and he might not come back and whatever shall I do? Well I didn't know what to say, so I just like tries to jolly her a bit, and it all comes out, that he asked her and she says no, and now she's wondering if she wouldn't ha' done better to say yes.'

Another long silence, a pull of beer, and then the voice continued. 'None of us never saw him again. He was killed overseas, poor young gentleman, and when the news come poor Aggie went all to pieces. She cried and she cried, and cook scolded and Mr Mayhew, the butler, had to tell the mistress she had the infuenza cause she couldn't ha' waited at table, not looking like she did. And any time she wasn't on duty she'd run off to the apple loft and sit there rocking back and forth and crying. I went to her once and said Lord, Miss, don't take on so, and she said, she kept thinking how she'd said no to him, and he'd gone away to his death without her love.'

He sniffed deeply and sighed at the memory, and drained his pint, and looked so mournfully into its depths that Gerry hastened to offer him another one.

'Well,' he said when he brought it back and placed it before the old man, 'that's very interesting, what you've told me. I wonder if—'

'Do yew want the rest of the story, or don't yew?' Mr Swainson asked aggressively.

'Oh yes, of course. I'm sorry, I thought you'd finished. Please go on.'

'Well, the rest of the story won't take long. I heard some of it afterwards, and some of it—well, you'll see. It seems poor Aggie went a bit strange after that, and started having nightmares and walking in her sleep and all that sort of caper. Next thing I hears there's a big fuss up at the house cause one of the maids has gone and got herself pregnant. Well, when I hears that it's Aggie, I'm taken all aback, cause if ever anyone was heart-whole for one man, that was her. Anyway I'm in the kitchen one day, bringing in the veg, when there's a terrible wailing and screaming from upstairs, and Cook says Lord, whatever may that be, and after a while Mr Mayhew comes down shaking his head and rubbing his hands and he says that poor girl has taken leave of her wits. And Cook says whatever do you mean, and he looks at me like as to say, not in front of the boy, and he takes her to one side and tells her. He didn't mean me to hear, but I picked it up, some of it then and some of it later. It seems that the mistress was for turning Aggie out when she finds she's pregnant, until Aggie starts up to crying and swearing on the Bible that she never laid with no one, and that it's the Holy Ghost that has put her in the family way.'

Gerry spilt his beer, and mopped it up extremely carefully with beer mats.

'Of course,' he said in a voice that barely trembled, 'no one believed her, I suppose?'

'Course they didn't. But she went on so about it, and got so bad, that in the end they decided she wasn't right in the head, and the mistress said they couldn't turn her away in that state, so they locked her up in one of the attic bedrooms till they could decide what to do with her.'

'Poor girl,' Gerry said involuntarily.

'Poor girl is right,' Mr Swainson said approvingly. 'I felt terrible bad for her. I could see her sometimes from the orchard, looking out of the little window, her face so white pressed against the window-pane, and I suffered terrible bad for her. So one evening I climbed up the ilex tree what grew on that side of the house and I swung across on to the gable roof and got up the roof tree to her window, for to give her some apples. Lord, I never seen such a change in a girl. She looked like an old woman, she did, and her eyes all blackened from weeping.' He shook his head sadly. 'So when she asked me to help her, what could I say?'

'I should think you'd say yes,' Gerry said, a response seeming needed.

'That's right. I said I'd help her. God forgive me. If I'd ha' known what would happen—but then no one never knows, do they? You can only do what seems right at the time. Yes, God forgive me, I said I'd help her.'

* * *

Gerry finished his careful report to Polly.

'I don't know what conclusions we can draw from all this. I think it would be dangerous to draw too many, and yet, on the other hand, it is difficult to avoid drawing some. The old man was obviously telling the truth, he had no reason to lie, and he recognized the photograph at once without prompting as being Captain Hammond. Above all, I have to leave it to your discretion how much and when to tell Agatha. I am so glad she has consented at last to go into a nursing home. She so obviously needs care and attention, and the money mustn't be a consideration. I have lots of discreet uncles I can borrow from if necessary.'

He rested his aching hand: he wasn't used to writing such volumes long-hand. His mind was filled with the images conjured up so vividly by the old man's dry and colourless voice. It was as if he was watching a cinema film, only in this film he was all the actors too. He could feel the quality of terror of the parlour-maid, locked up in the attic of that great dour house, convinced she was being haunted from beyond the grave by the man she had refused to give herself to; pregnant, terrified, reviled by all, locked up as mad and blasphemous, alone and friendless.

And the boy, impressionable, imaginative, the mother's pet and therefore probably more sensitive to women's emotions than his sturdier brothers; seeing the white face at the window, seeing himself as her rescuer. Probably he was more than half in love with her—he must have been about fifteen by then. And the terrifying escape, at the dead of night, with nothing but moonlight and a rope to help, the woman, ungainly with child, and the slight, narrow-chested boy, climbing out of the window, across the treacherous roofs, and down the dark ilex to safety. The moon going in, the clouds sweeping across to hide them with shadow as they stumbled through the orchard to the temporary haven of the barn, the apple loft where she had met her lover through a long, hot, drowsy summer.

The girl, alone in the loft after the boy had run off home; he knew he could not even begin to imagine her terror as the birth-pains began, her anguish as she gave birth alone in that dark loft.

Perhaps by morning she was mercifully

feverish. It would have been close, humid, with the gathering storm; perhaps she was hardly aware of the unnatural darkness, the rumbling of thunder overhead, the vivid, blue, briny flashes of lightning. They say you never see the one that strikes you. There would have been a tremendous bang as the tree split, and then a long, groaning crash as it fell, smashing through the roof of the barn, bringing the beams down through the apple loft where the woman lay with her baby. She would perhaps have known little about it.

But the boy would have known when he came back the next day and saw the splintered ruins of the barn. How could he find the words to tell them? Trembling, almost out of his mind with fear and apprehension he must have been, as he watched them digging in the wreckage for the woman he had tried to help, bringing out her shattered body. And the baby no one wanted.

He turned again to his letter. 'I wish you could have seen that poor old man. He really cared for that woman, you know. He must have suffered all his life, thinking it was all his fault. He looked as brittle as a dry reed.' Holding himself so carefully upright, so still, as if he were filled with pain even yet. 'I think Agatha shouldn't be worried by it all yet, but you will know better than I do on that score.'

She was near her time, and shouldn't be upset. He finished off the letter and stuck it down, stamped it, and trotted down to the porter's lodge to post it, and then, needing the fresh air, he went out for a walk. When he came back, he decided on impulse to phone up Agatha and see how she was. She was so much on his mind, and she might be giving birth any time now.

Ten minutes later he was frantically dialling Polly's number, praying she would be in.

'Polly, thank God, it's Gerry. I've just phoned the nursing home. Agatha isn't there . . . I don't know. She must have gone home. They said she discharged herself three days ago . . . They couldn't, they could only advise. Listen, for God's sake go round there and see if she's all right. I've got this terrible feeling . . . Well, phone if you like, but for God's sake make sure she's all right. I'm coming down as soon as I can. I'm leaving right away. Yes, I think so.'

* * *

All gone now. She was alone again, and this time for ever. They had tried to shut her up, imprison her, but she had escaped and come home, for only here was any comfort. Here He had been; now He had left her too. Her life had contracted to this one room, dim and blood-smelling, and this one point of time, near the end.

And the baby. It was sleeping now, its

mouth slack around her nipple, its belly tight with her milk. She had been afraid, but now the fear was gone, the pain was over, and there was only the waiting. She thought of her mother, waiting in that room she saw sometimes, listening to the V-1s overhead. They say they sounded like two-stroke engines, little slow mopeds chugging along in the sky above you; and when the engine cut out, they fell. Sometimes they would glide for miles before they came to earth; other times, they would tilt their noses and drop like a stone. When you heard them you held your breath, praying they would pass you by and kill someone else; and if the engine stopped, your heart contracted with fear as you waited for the blast, for death.

She understood now. It had all happened before. He had come to her, mistaking her for her mother, demanding love. And her mother—could she have escaped? There was always the possibility; but there was also the baby. *Let me resign my life for this life*. Was it not that which they all sought, the martyrs, the soldiers, the rebels, the lovers, something that would be more important to you than yourself, something in which to sink your identity and all the aching, wearying, frightening responsibility for it? A cause, a reason, something bigger than you that would blot out the doubts and the glimpses of emptiness underneath. So when the time came she had—

not even chosen, had just done it—had saved the child with her own life.

It had all happened before.

She looked down at the sleeping baby; a baby's amorphous features, but there was something distantly, hauntingly familiar about her, little screwed-up face under the dark thatch of birth-hair. She did not look like Him. He had left her; she had loved Him, and He had gone away and left her to be alone again and for ever, but now there was the baby who had come from nowhere and did not look like Him at all. She looked like

Agatha

she looked like Agatha

she looked like

The woman's mind gaped, chaos yawned wider and wider, engulfing her. She looked down at the baby in her arms and she *knew*. She understood all now, and understanding was madness

because it was herself

she had given birth to

Agatha herself that baby was herself and now oh God it would all start all over again it had all happened before that was funny she could laugh that she had said that to herself and not realized and this child was doomed already to go through everything again the fear and the pain and the madness because it was

herself

She knew why her mother had died (why she

had died) and not saved herself. They could not both live, but in the end some things were stronger than reason. I died and let you live though I knew that I condemned you (myself)

there was no choice. Seeking, always seeking, something that would be more important than myself, sought it through religion, sought it through love, found it, in the end, in my daughter, my daughter.

And there was the irony.

How dark it was outside. Would there be a storm? Resign my life for this life. Oh my daughter. Love. Love me.

The rumbling began, somewhere distant, growing louder.

I am Agatha. Agatha.

She folded the baby closer in her arms, shielding it with her body, as if love could hold off the chaos outside.

And overhead, the engine stopped.

Evening Standard 5.4.79

A two-day-old baby girl was rescued by firemen today after an explosion wrecked her home in west London.
Her mother, the only other occupant of the house, was killed by the blast, which is thought to have been caused by a gas leak.
Story Page 3

* * *

The baby cried, had been crying almost non-stop. She lay in the carrycot a neighbour had lent on the sofa in Polly's flat, her face and fists screwed up in the effort, it seemed to Polly, to break all records for infant yelling.

'Perhaps she's hungry. Do you think she's hungry?' Gerry said hopefully.

'Oh Lord, how would I know? I don't know anything about babies.' She heard the unspoken question, and said fretfully, 'Well we couldn't let her be taken away by strangers, could we?'

'Shall we make up a bottle for her, then? Perhaps she's hungry. Have you got those instructions that woman wrote out for you?'

The baby's yells redoubled, and both reached out simultaneously, their hands colliding in mid-air. Polly shrugged and drew back, and Gerry touched the baby's hand with his forefinger. It uncurled like a starfish and closed around his finger and the yelling faltered. He stared down at it, and his heart ached with pity.

'And now it will all start, all over again,' he said!

'We mustn't let it, that's all,' Polly said fiercely. Her own maternal protectiveness amazed her. She could never have thought herself capable of feeling such emotion towards what she had always thought was basically no more than a pair of defecating lungs, but this baby was different. She loved it, she wanted it. It was something to put into the emptiness inside. 'We mustn't let it.'

'How can we possibly stop it?' he said. The baby stopped crying abruptly, and the silence was blissful.

'Well, for a start, we won't let her be brought up in an institution. We'll bring her up ourselves.'

Gerry gave his other forefinger to the other fist. The baby opened her eyes.

'And for another thing, we won't call her Agatha,' Polly said.

Gerry looked up, appalled, and their eyes met above the cot.

'But that's who she is,' he said.